# CORBIN BLEU
## Up Close

**DEE SCOTT**

An original publication of Pocket Books

POCKET BOOKS, a division of Simon & Schuster, Inc.
1230 Avenue of the Americas, New York, NY 10020

DOWNTOWN
BOOKWORKS INC.
PRODUCED BY DOWNTOWN BOOKWORKS INC.
President: JULIE MERBERG
Senior Vice President: PATTY BROWN
Editor: SARAH PARVIS

Designed by REDDISH-BLUE (WWW.REDDISH-BLUE.COM)

Library of Congress Cataloging-in-Publication is available
ISBN-13: 978-1-4165-4114-1
ISBN-10: 1-4165-4114-4
This Pocket Books trade paperback edition December 2006
10 9 8 7 6 5 4 3 2 1
POCKET and colophon are registered trademarks of Simon & Schuster, Inc.
Manufactured in the United States of America

For information regarding special discounts for bulk purchases,
please contact Simon & Schuster Special Sales at 1-800-456-6798
or business@simonandschuster.com

PHOTO Credits:
All photos supplied and © The Reivers family
with the following exceptions:
Grettel Cortes: Front Cover, 2, 76 TR,
80 BL, 87 BL, 93 L, 96, Back Cover;
Gale Sherrodd: 39 TL, 41 BR;
CATCH THAT KID © Twentieth Century Fox
all rights reserved: 38 BR, 40 TL, 40 BL, 42.

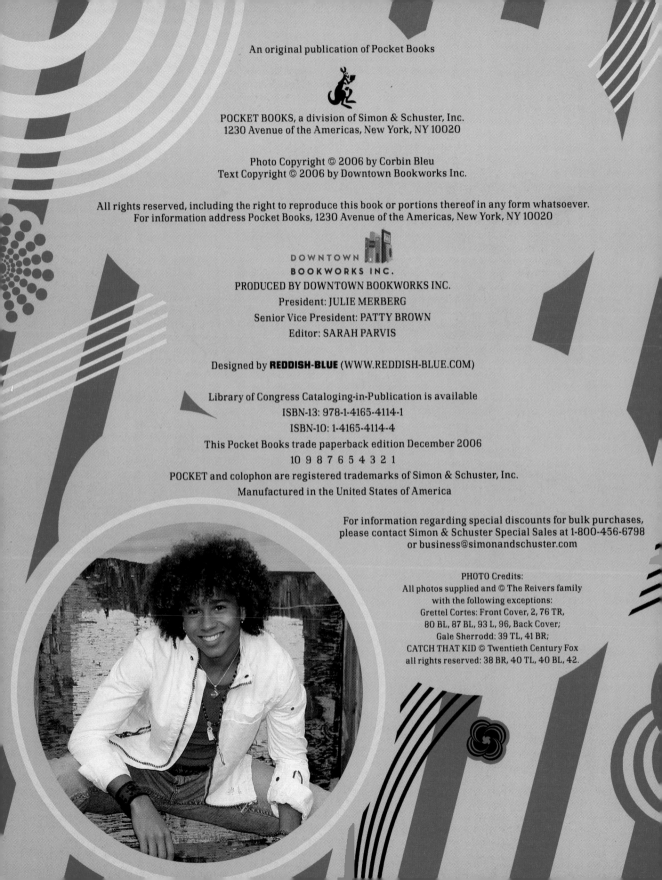

# CORBIN BLEU

## UP CLOSE

DEE SCOTT

Produced by DOWNTOWN BOOKWORKS INC.

POCKET BOOKS

NEW YORK    LONDON    TORONTO    SYDNEY

I would like to thank some people who have played very important roles in this journey.

First, I would like to thank God, for without Him nothing would be possible.

All my fans, for your encouragement and support.

The wonderful teachers I have had over the years, especially, Leslie Rugg, Kimberly Taweel, Betsy Becker, Laura Beyer, Ardie Bryant, and Doc Simpson. Julia Gregory, I promise to breathe.

The staff and faculty of the Los Angeles County High School for the Arts, especially Lois Hunter, Gale Sherrodd, David Nathan Schwartz, Dr. Odell Scott, and Jill Walker.

Lynn Raines-Levy, Paul Levy, Jennifer Raines, and Jeffrey Raines.

Bonnie Liedtke, Brandy Gold, Thor Bradwell, and everyone at TalentWorks Agency.

Ms. Debbie Allen and the staff and faculty at the Debbie Allen Dance Academy, who raise the bar.

Patsy Metzger. Randy James. Scott Appel and all my event buds.

Grettel Cortes, my favorite photographer.

My partners in crime from CATCH THAT KID: Kristen Stewart, Max Thieriot, and Bart Freundlich.

Sarah Parvis and my friends at Downtown Bookworks Inc. Designer Andy Capelli.

Aunt Maria and Uncle Bill. Richie, Cathy, and Maria. Tia Mechi. Uncle Joseph. Tia Emily.

To my aunts, uncles, and cousins: I love you all.

Grandma Sarah. My great grandparents, Grace and Arnold Mitchell.

Ms. Doreen, the Angarano family, and everyone at Reflections In Dance.

Carl and the Lindner family. The Maldanado family. The Shrode family. The Gaines family.

The Wallengren family. Gary LeRoi Gray and Tracy Avance. Jerry Kernion.

Whitney Ackerman. Dan Rivero. Eric Feig and Michael Golland. UMG.

The wonderful cast and crew of FLIGHT 29 DOWN, especially

Hallee, Lauren, Kristy, Allen, Jeremy, Johnny, and show creator D.J. MacHale.

Stan Rogow, you are the best, I love you. Elliot Lurie, thank you for believing in me.

My HIGH SCHOOL MUSICAL posse:

Zac, Vanessa, Ashley, Lucas, Monique, Ryne, Chris, Olesya, Alyson, Bart, Chuckie,

Bonnie, and the amazing Kenny Ortega. Barry Rosenbush, Bill Borden, and Don Schain.

Rich Ross, Gary Marsh, Judy Taylor, and the rest of my extended family at the Disney Channel.

Bob Cavallo, Jon Lind, and Hollywood Records.

Paul Hoen and the wonderful Toronto crew and cast of JUMP IN!

All the unnamed trainers, cast-mates, casting directors, producers, directors, assistants, agents, and extended family and friends who have helped and supported me along the way.

The incomparable Dee Scott, whose vision and hard work has made this book possible.

And of course, the thank you that I am most proud to say: my incredible family.

Mom, Dad, Hunter, Phoenix, and Jag, I love you guys so much.

Without you, I would not be who I am today.

Thank you for all of the wonderful years of love and support

that you have given me. I will cherish them for life.

# CONTENTS

from the library of

Cameron Stanley

This book is dedicated in loving memory
to my grandparents, Joseph and Theresa Callari.
You are always in my heart.

Hi!

Many of you know me as Nathan on the TV series FLIGHT 29 DOWN. And a lot of you recognize me as Chad from the Disney Channel movie HIGH SCHOOL MUSICAL. But I wanted to let you all get to know me as Corbin, just Corbin.

So I sat down with my parents, David and Martha Reivers, and my little sisters, Hunter, Phoenix, and Jag, and we pulled out all our family photo albums. We selected our favorite snapshots, and lots of memories came flooding back. We spent hours talking and laughing about when we lived in Brooklyn, NY, about our move to Los Angeles, about family, friends, and all the adventures I've had along the way. We put them all together in this very personal, very special book—a book I want to share with my fans!

On the following pages you'll see baby pictures of me, shots of my family, shots of me at school and in my own "high school musicals" like FOOTLOOSE and GREASE, and lots of photos of my friends and co-stars from FLIGHT 29 DOWN, HIGH SCHOOL MUSICAL, and other popular TV shows and movies—fellow actors like Zac Efron, Ashley Tisdale, Vanessa Anne Hudgens, Lauren Storm, Miley Cyrus, and even George Clooney, to name a few!

You'll read about how I first got started at the age of two doing print ads and TV commercials, about my school days, dance classes, and my first lead role in the movie CATCH THAT KID. And, of course, I couldn't leave out a front-row-center and behind-the-scenes look at HIGH SCHOOL MUSICAL. It's all been amazing. Hopefully you will like to come along with me for more—my upcoming Disney Channel movie, JUMP IN!, with Keke (AKEELAH AND THE BEE) Palmer, and a very special project I am working on right now: my debut CD from Hollywood Records.

I had a lot of fun putting this book together to let you know the things that are important to me and that make me smile. And I hope this book will make YOU smile.

Thanks for everything!

Peace & Love,

# IN THE SPOTLIGHT

*Corbin saw a huge HIGH SCHOOL MUSICAL poster at The Grove in Los Angeles. It hadn't opened yet, and he knew it was going to be hot!*

Corbin Bleu fans: Alert! This is the official, totally authorized story of one of the hottest rising stars of today: Corbin Bleu. He, of course, is best known as Chad in the mega-hit HIGH SCHOOL MUSICAL. But he is no overnight success story. He's been working and honing his talents for nearly his entire life. If you are a true-blue Bleu fan, you've probably already devoured all of the magazine pieces on him and scoured the Web for the inside scoop on his career and personality. Well, you don't have to go any further in your Corbin Bleu quest. On the following pages, you'll read about and see his life unfold from baby pictures to remembrances of his first days in school; from photos of school productions to his parents' tales of Corbin growing up; the personal stories of his landing roles in the films, MYSTERY MEN, GALAXY QUEST, and CATCH THAT KID, and the behind-the-scenes bonding with the cast of TV's FLIGHT 29 DOWN. And, of course, you'll get the inside story on the show that took his already hot career and catapulted it into hyperspace: HIGH SCHOOL MUSICAL.

When HIGH SCHOOL MUSICAL debuted on Friday night, January 20, 2006, it broke every ratings record for a Disney Channel original movie in the network's entire thirteen-year history. That first airing, seen by over 7 million viewers, outpaced anything that'd come before, including the mega-popular hits, THE LIZZIE MCGUIRE MOVIE, TWITCHES, and THE CHEETAH GIRLS.

The premiere was only the beginning.

HIGH SCHOOL MUSICAL aired all weekend long, and with each successive showing, the exuberant song-and-dance-fest picked up steam—more viewers, more records broken, more blogs, text messages, IMs, more everything. The buzz-o-meter was off the charts. Within weeks, it shot from "most popular Disney TV movie" to a true pop-culture phenomenon. Translation: everybody's hearing about it, talking about it, writing about it—and reenacting it.

Within six months, it'd spawned a top-selling DVD and a chart-busting CD, earned six Emmy nominations, and won the prestigious Television Critics Association Award for Outstanding Children's Programming. In what seemed like lightning speed, teen magazines hit the shelves with cover stories and huge color pinups of the stars, and even mags aimed at adults covered it. (NEWSWEEK did a ten-page story!) Most importantly, in terms of spreading the word, HIGH SCHOOL MUSICAL fans' websites and blogs sprung up like wildfire so kids all over the world could share HSM info 24/7!

*"I was the worst out of everybody at basketball," reveals Corbin about his HIGH SCHOOL MUSICAL b-ball boot camp. But he got the hang of it!*

9

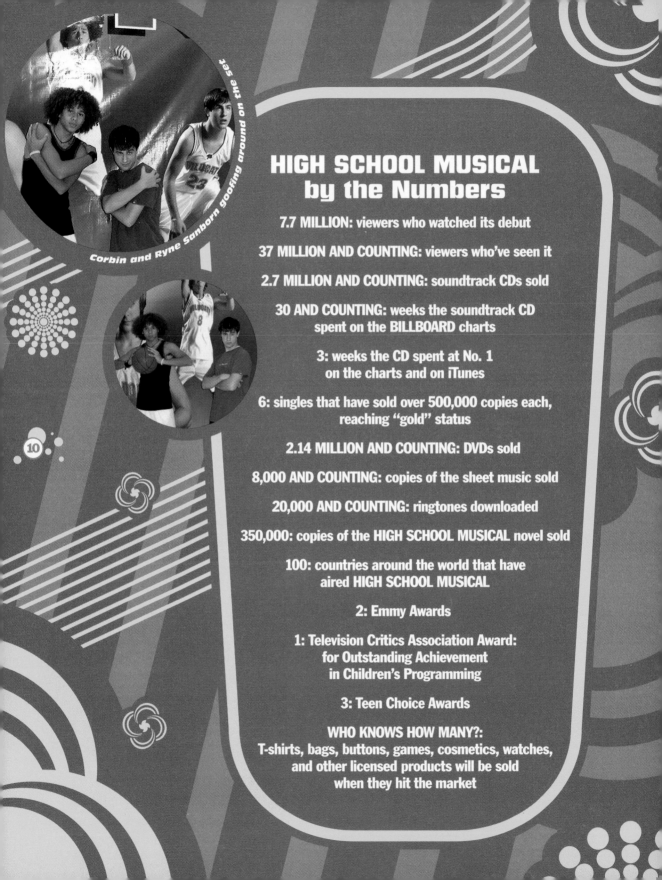

*Corbin and Ryne Sanborn goofing around on the set*

# HIGH SCHOOL MUSICAL
# by the Numbers

**7.7 MILLION:** viewers who watched its debut

**37 MILLION AND COUNTING:** viewers who've seen it

**2.7 MILLION AND COUNTING:** soundtrack CDs sold

**30 AND COUNTING:** weeks the soundtrack CD
spent on the BILLBOARD charts

**3:** weeks the CD spent at No. 1
on the charts and on iTunes

**6:** singles that have sold over 500,000 copies each,
reaching "gold" status

**2.14 MILLION AND COUNTING:** DVDs sold

**8,000 AND COUNTING:** copies of the sheet music sold

**20,000 AND COUNTING:** ringtones downloaded

**350,000:** copies of the HIGH SCHOOL MUSICAL novel sold

**100:** countries around the world that have
aired HIGH SCHOOL MUSICAL

**2:** Emmy Awards

**1:** Television Critics Association Award:
for Outstanding Achievement
in Children's Programming

**3:** Teen Choice Awards

**WHO KNOWS HOW MANY?:**
T-shirts, bags, buttons, games, cosmetics, watches,
and other licensed products will be sold
when they hit the market

For those truly in the know, the HIGH SCHOOL MUSICAL express actually took off a few weeks before the film's debut—on December 31, 2005. Fans got a special sneak peak of the cast when they performed some of the musical numbers on the Disney Channel's New Year's Eve special. From there, the HIGH SCHOOL MUSICAL phenomenon took off. Free downloads of the song "Breaking Free" were offered, and music videos were broadcast on the network. The online music blitz was followed by the HIGH SCHOOL MUSICAL soundtrack CD, officially released on January 10, 2006. Radio Disney played songs from the soundtrack on its stations around the country, and Disneychannel.com posted song lyrics. Fans could even sign up for a HIGH SCHOOL MUSICAL Party Kit, so they could host their own sleepover sing-alongs.

By the time the movie actually aired, countless kids knew the "who's who" of the cast, the words to the catchy tunes, and even some of the dance moves. And by the time the movie aired, Corbin Bleu's rising star was traveling faster than the speed of light!

Okay, it's confession time: Even Corbin and his cast-mates didn't realize how huge HIGH SCHOOL MUSICAL would become—not right away, anyhow. When they first auditioned, each actor got to see only a few pages of the script (in showbiz lingo they're called "sides") with the scenes for their individual tryouts. By the time he was offered his part, Corbin had read the script and loved it, but he still hadn't seen the music. It wasn't until the cast was smack in the middle of filming that it began to dawn on them—wait, this could be something huge!

## So, What's the Story?

Priming fans for an upcoming movie and creating all the buzz in the world, however, doesn't guarantee a hit. So what exactly did make HIGH SCHOOL MUSICAL the smash hit it became? There's gotta be more to the story.

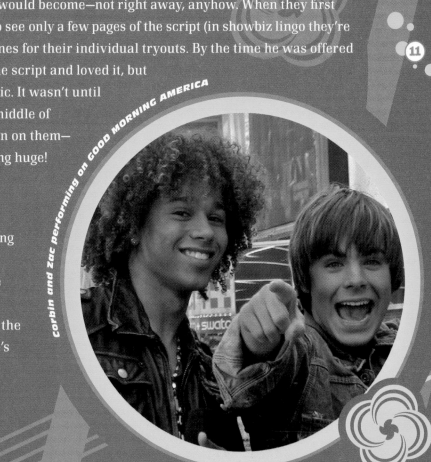

Corbin and Zac performing on GOOD MORNING AMERICA

The cast lived and worked in Utah—their trailers were set against a majestic mountain skyline.

The story itself, however, is a good place to start.

On the simplest level, the tale is a classic. You've seen and heard it before in movies, books, TV shows, songs, and dances. Boy meets girl; they are complete opposites, but against all odds, they fall for each other. The romance doesn't go smoothly. Friends and family on both sides refuse to accept the two as a couple and try to sabotage the budding relationship. In the end…well, in the unforgettable case of ROMEO AND JULIET or WEST SIDE STORY, it didn't go so well! In movie musicals like GREASE, however, the gaga couple lived happily ever after. Or at least long enough for a sequel and spin-offs!

HIGH SCHOOL MUSICAL is the tale of a basketball-playing dreamboat named Troy Bolton and the beautiful but shy new kid in school, Gabriella Montez. Troy and Gabriella meet randomly during winter break, when their families end up vacationing at the same ski resort near Salt Lake City, Utah. It happens to be (romantic timing alert!) New Year's Eve, and during the resort's cheesy karaoke session, they're called up to sing together.

Neither of them is into it, but once in the spotlight, they cave. Something amazing happens when they sing together. But all good things (and vacations) must come to an end. And soon enough, they exchange cell phone snapshots and digits, and go their separate ways, probably never to see each other again.

Except…not so fast…Gabriella's mom is transferred to Albuquerque, New Mexico. It turns out that that's where Troy lives and reigns supreme as the No. 1 high school hottie. He's captain of the Wildcats basketball team, he's popular, and he's best friends with everyone, especially teammate Chad, his closest confidant. Troy and Chad exemplify the jocks. They hang

Corbin and Monique practice their moves with director Kenny Ortega.

*Wrap it up! Chris, Ashley, Vanessa, Corbin, and Zac celebrate a job well done at the wrap party for HIGH SCHOOL MUSICAL.*

out with cheerleaders and win their games. No one sings, no one dances, no one cooks, designs clothes, or even *thinks* of joining the drama club. They dribble, they pass, they shoot, they score. And they like it that way.

Gabriella, the brainiac babe, is quickly admitted into the science and math clique, led by Taylor. In her, they see a way to nail their Scholastic Decathlon. Acceptance into that group is OK with Gabriella, and she works hard to be part of the team and to help them ace their upcoming competition. They, too, are a closed and focused circle—not open to slackers, drama club kids, and especially not open to jocks.

Troy and Gabriella might not even see each other in school, except they end up in the same homeroom. Their teacher, Mrs. Darbus, runs the drama club. She's currently organizing the school's winter musical, and (dramatically!) urges students to audition. In fact, Ms. Darbus' passion for theater is matched only by the basketball coach's obsession with sports and his winning team. The basketball coach (did we not mention?) also doubles as Troy's proud pop. He dismisses theater; Ms. Darbus derides sports. It's a scenario that's been the norm for East High since …well, as long as anyone can remember.

And, as the saying goes, if it ain't broke, don't try to fix it.

13

*At the wrap party at the Governor's Mansion in Utah, Corbin and the cast are all looking forward to the movie's debut!*

Corbin leans on his very own official
HIGH SCHOOL MUSICAL chair.

That's certainly the attitude of the sister and brother duo Sharpay and Ryan Evans; they've starred in every play and musical since they've been at East High. This new one won't be any different if they have anything to say—or sing—about it! Of course, fair is fair, and the bro-sis pair is required to audition along with the others who think they can handle the lead in the duet competition.

The school's status quo is thrown way off-kilter when Troy and Gabriella witness the stagey siblings being cruel to the musical's pianist and end up singing together—reliving their great vacation karaoke duet. And before you can say "Breaking Free," Troy and Gabriella find themselves in official competition with Sharpay and Ryan for the musical leads. Not only that, but Troy and Gabriella are busted, as word gets back to their groups that they've…accidentally on purpose…auditioned for a musical. Both camps, the Wildcats and the Decathelons, come back with two words: not cool.

On the set with Chris Warren Jr.

Enter Corbin's character, Chad. This guy lives and breathes basketball. When he finds out his best friend and the captain of his winning team has gotten himself wrapped up in a musical, he starts scheming. And Chad's not the only one! The warring factions band together to derail Troy and Gabriella's chances of winning the leads …and sabotage their blossoming romance. Things get out of hand fast, and Chad is the first to realize that the cliques have gone too far.

It takes true teamwork, a display of real friendship, and playing to each group's strengths to bring about a happy ending. Everyone dances away a winner in HIGH SCHOOL MUSICAL. How do they do that? As the theme song says, "We're all in this together!" Even Sharpay and Ryan get caught up in the infectious goodwill as the East High kids get their heads into a new game.

14

Ryne, Corbin, Zac, and Chris
hanging out

An upbeat, uplifting, and satisfying story will always be meaningful, but that's not the entire reason for HIGH SCHOOL MUSICAL's resounding success. For where there's a good, solid story, there's usually a walloping subtext—a message that touches everyone.

## The Message in the Music

"It's all about high school cliques. Kids feel pressure and they always want to fit in. HIGH SCHOOL MUSICAL showed that you can step out of the box that cliques put you in, and show the rest of the world that you can do something different than what you're known for."

Corbin explains, "With Troy, he plays basketball. That is what he has always done—his dad taught him that. He wanted something more, and he was able to step outside and sing. So the message for kids is that you need to follow your dream. You need to do what you want and not worry about what other people say, or who tries to bring you down."

In interviews with SCHOLASTIC NEWS ONLINE, the other cast members agree. Zac Efron, who plays Troy, says: "You have to be yourself, walk your own path. Don't listen to all the pressures that come from the outside world." Vanessa Anne Hudgens, who plays Gabriella, adds, "The message of HIGH SCHOOL MUSICAL is: conquer your fears."

Corbin wants you to know that we're all in this together

In the same interview, Ashley Tisdale, so *sharp* as Sharpay, puts it this way: "You don't have to be just one thing. Kids can get stuck in a clique and can't get out of it. You feel people won't support you in anything else. It's important to find yourself in school and be happy about it, and if people don't support you, they're not your real friends."

That theme is timeless; it reaches out to everyone, everywhere.

15

## The Kickin' Cast and Its Director

Corbin offers another interesting reason for HIGH SCHOOL MUSICAL's astounding success: It was the right cast, at the right time, in the right movie. Everyone in the cast was a working actor, but except for Ashley, they all were unknowns at that point. Not one cast member was a household name. "I think that helped draw the audience," he says, "because they didn't have presumptions about us. If someone like Hilary Duff were in the film, there'd be a preconceived notion—they know her as Lizzie McGuire, or as Hilary, a star. Whereas with us, they just saw our characters, and were able to relate to that more."

Corbin teaches some of the moves to "Get'cha Head in the Game."

HIGH SCHOOL MUSICAL had a timeless tale, a cool cast, and a meaningful message, but what *really* knocked it out of the box, of course, was the music—the tunes and the moves, the catchy songs, snappy dances, and eye-poppin' performances. HIGH SCHOOL MUSICAL's team of writers, producers, stylists, casting directors, editors, composers, and musicians was top-tier, but some serious kudos have to go to director-choreographer, Kenny Ortega. "Kenny is very cool," asserts Corbin, "because he's a dancer, he's able to see things from a musical point of view."

The HIGH SCHOOL MUSICAL cast appears on the TODAY show. "Oh, man, that was crazy," says Corbin. "It was insane. It felt like we were The Beatles. We walked out, and it was just hundreds of screaming people. We'd go up and try to shake their hands, and they'd try and pull you into the crowd!"

16

Kenny Ortega gave the HSM cast special T-shirts
during a night out at one of their favorite
Italian restaurants, Buca di Beppo.

## The AMERICAN IDOL Factor

What's AMERICAN IDOL got to do with HIGH SCHOOL MUSICAL? A little thing called zeitgeist. The term (pronounced ZITE-guyst) roughly translates into, "what is happening in the pop culture world" or "the trends and fads that have got everyone excited." Clearly, AMERICAN IDOL is part of the current American zeitgeist. The idea of auditioning, of getting your shot at becoming a singer, and the reality that "anyone can become a star" are extra-powerful right now.

Corbin explains the connection: "AMERICAN IDOL helped to bring musicals back to popularity. There was a time when everyone was talking about GREASE and FAME and FOOTLOOSE. Then, for a while, musicals kind of died down. Later there were the movies, MOULIN ROUGE, CHICAGO, RENT, and THE PRODUCERS. With the success of those, boosted by AMERICAN IDOL, and now with HIGH SCHOOL MUSICAL—which was an original as opposed to something being redone—I'm pretty sure you're going to be seeing a lot more!"

So, be prepared: The HIGH SCHOOL MUSICAL phenomenon is alive and well—and shows no signs of slowing down soon. And neither does Corbin Bleu!

# FAMILY TIES

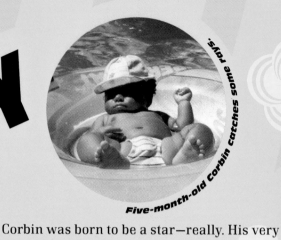

*Five-month-old Corbin catches some rays.*

Corbin was born to be a star—really. His very
entrance into the world, on February 21, 1989, was dramatic.
Or rather, comedic. As his family tells it, it was like a classic
I LOVE LUCY episode. The setting was Corbin's parents' apartment
in the Sunset Park section of Brooklyn, New York, and the players included
his very pregnant mom, Martha; his dad, David; his maternal grandfather, Joseph Callari,
who was up on a tall ladder installing a ceiling fan; Martha's best friend, Mercedes Paris;
and Mercedes' sister, Dulce Toribio, who'd come over with an herbal drink. According to
Mercedes' mom, who'd had twelve children, the special ginger-root drink she brought was
supposed to bring on labor. Martha's due date was the next day, and since she had been
sick throughout most of her pregnancy, she was willing to try anything to get things going.

"It was so hilarious," Mercedes
remembers, "because no one really thought
it was going to work. But sure enough, four
hours later, she suddenly went into labor.
It happened so quickly, we were all staring
at her in utter shock. Everybody went into
panic mode. David was running around.
Martha's begging us to let her take a shower
so she could wash her hair. We were like, 'Are
you crazy?' And all this time, we're running
around like chickens without our heads—

**Martha and David knew they were blessed when
they had Corbin—and it was proved when they
played his birth date and weight on a NY State
Lottery ticket right after he was born...and
won $200!**

**David and Martha Reivers in Jamaica**

running underneath and around the ladder—because her father wouldn't come down. He continued to install the fan, saying, 'Oh, everything's going to be alright. This is her first baby. She's got a long way to go.' And sure enough, we rushed her to the hospital. It was freezing in February, the dead of winter—and after all that, Corbin wasn't born until the next day, exactly on his due date."

Corbin's mom puts it best: "He was special from the beginning. He was a blessing."

Straight up, you can see that Corbin's from a tight family with very close and caring friends. The famous HIGH SCHOOL MUSICAL ender, "We're All in This Together," could be the family's theme song. For Corbin, it really is all about family—togetherness, support, a whole lot of memories, laughter, and love.

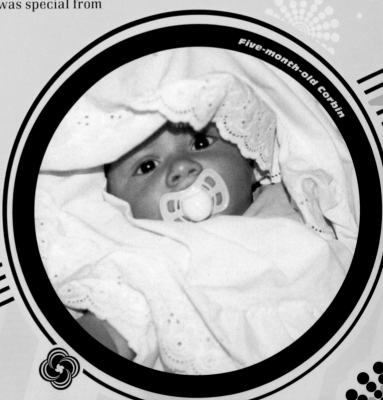

Five-month-old Corbin

The family's story begins in Brooklyn, New York.

Corbin's mom, Martha Callari, was the youngest of seven kids in a large, traditional Italian family. Like her siblings (including two sets of twins), Martha attended a neighborhood Catholic school. From her earliest years, she demonstrated a definite talent for, and interest in, acting and dancing. Like the little ham that son Corbin would turn out to be, she too was a born performer. Martha dreamed of attending New York's High School of Performing Arts, the school that inspired the musical FAME. The auditions to get in were, and are, demanding—a long shot at best for most hopefuls. Thousands of talented kids compete for fewer than 300 spots.

Corbin is a stocking stuffer!

"Martha was taking private lessons with a dance teacher," Mercedes recalls, "and had worked up a beautiful routine for the audition. When she did get accepted, it was huge—a very big deal for her."

It was an even bigger deal for her fearful mother, Theresa Callari, who worried about her daughter venturing out of the neighborhood parochial school to travel on the subways into Manhattan by herself to go to the High School of Performing Arts. "Her mother was adamant," remembers Mercedes. "She wanted her to continue to go to Catholic school. It was pretty dramatic. Can you imagine? She prepared so hard for it, but her mom had so many reservations." It took a combined, concerted effort by friends and family—including Martha's older siblings—to convince Mrs. Callari to allow Martha to go to the school of her dreams.

*Corbin and his dad in their backyard in Brooklyn*

Corbin's dad, David Reivers, grew up in the city of Kingston, on the beautiful Caribbean island of Jamaica. When David was ten years old, he and his brother joined his mom in the United States. David spent the rest of his childhood in Coney Island, New York. Throughout his school years, he was a sporty guy. Though talented at many games, his undeniable favorite was football. By the time he enrolled in Kingsboro Community College, David realized that any hope he harbored of making a living playing sports wasn't realistic—he just wasn't a big enough guy to go pro.

He started college as a business major but eventually found his way to the theater department. He admits, "I was first drawn there [as a way to meet] girls but eventually found a great love for theater and embraced it. Ever since then, I had what they call 'the bug.'"

*Corbin's First Halloween*

David started out performing in local theater and TV commercials. It was several years before he was able to quit his day job as a temp and make a living as an actor. As a young, struggling actor in New York City, David was always on the lookout for any opportunity to make it.

Meanwhile, Martha had graduated from high school and was working at a tanning salon, also on the lookout for any acting opportunities. A friend told her about a call for extras in a Japanese film, and she decided to go. While in line with dozens of other would-be extras, she tried to fill out her paperwork but realized that she didn't have a pen. Luckily, the guy behind her in line had one. That man was David Reivers. Martha looked up, and well…

"The minute David smiled, I fell in love," Martha said. "Corbin has his dad's smile—the most beautiful smile I've ever seen."

*One-year-old Corbin hangin' on the swings*

*Corbin's first Christmas*

After a few false starts—eighteen-year-old Martha didn't answer his calls at first and actually stood David up for their first two dates—the couple started dating. They eventually married and settled in Brooklyn, where Corbin was born and lived for the first seven years of his life.

His frequent babysitter and "adopted" Aunt Mercedes—whom he calls Tia Mechi—remembers, "I always thought he was going to have a legal career because he's such a negotiator. There would be times when I would say, 'OK, Corbin, it's time to go to bed.' And he'd go, 'Tia, can I have a drink of water? I'm really thirsty.' And I would say, 'Really? Because you just had a glass of water five minutes ago. Do you know how long ago that was?' He'd insist, 'I'm still very thirsty.' He would find ways to stay awake. He was only two or two and a half years old!"

A 21-month-old sports fan

Toddler Corbin soon displayed another talent: He was a brilliant little mimic, with a sponge-like ability to absorb what was happening around him. He was also an unabashed ham. By Corbin's own recollection, he was about two when he started to memorize lines to movies and TV shows. He loved it when he got to watch his dad work, or rehearse. By that time, David was an in-demand actor, often cast in commercials and guest-starring roles on TV shows. During Corbin's earliest years, David's credits included the TV show GABRIEL'S FIRE and the 1992 film MALCOLM X, starring Denzel Washington.

Corbin, age one, in the tub

Because Corbin showed an interest, and certainly had inherited the performing gene—"He doesn't have one shy bone in his body," his family agrees—David and Martha enrolled him in dance classes and were delighted to teach him about acting. Corbin remembers watching his father when he was about two years old. "My dad would say, 'What is the first rule for an actor or what does an actor do?' The most important rule was to listen. So, I would always listen. That was the first thing he taught me."

Corbin was so eager to learn more, to do more. "I would constantly memorize lines to movies and repeat them and act them out," he says. "That is when my folks were like, 'We've got to let him try this.'" His dad concurs. "We realized, 'Wow, this kid is smart.' As far as recognizing his talent, we knew from the age of two. He would book an audition, and we would work on the lines together. I remember thinking, 'That's great.' And saying to my wife, 'Honey, he's got it.'"

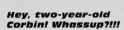
December 1989

Corbin's mom agrees. "His memorization was wonderful," she says.

His dad adds, "His sense of knowing how to deliver a line was just uncanny for—"

"—someone so small," Martha finishes the thought.

"It just really came easily to him," David marvels. "It was hard to watch and not go, 'How could you be this good?'" Corbin ended up getting offered many TV commercials. His parents aren't exactly sure which was first, but they do have fond memories of the one he did for Life cereal. "They had Corbin popping out of a box, so he didn't actually have to eat anything."

*Hey, two-year-old Corbin! Whassup?!!!*

In his toddler years, while other kids were learning to drink from a sippy cup, count to ten, and memorize their ABCs, this tiny tyke was doing all that and starring in commercials for such products as Bounty paper towels, Hasbro toys, and Nabisco cookies. Corbin thrived on his budding little career.

**"It was just very natural for me. I fell in love with it."**

What choice did his parents have, but to let him continue?

# A MODEL KID

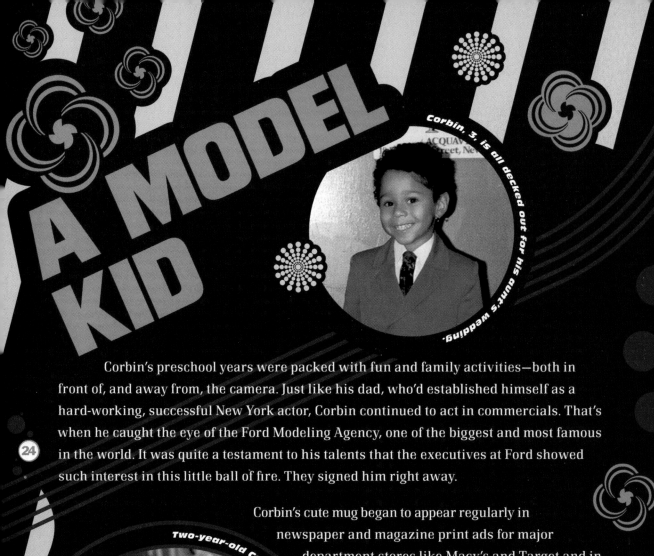

Corbin, 3, is all decked out for his aunt's wedding.

Two-year-old Corbin cleans up at Christmastime!

Corbin's preschool years were packed with fun and family activities—both in front of, and away from, the camera. Just like his dad, who'd established himself as a hard-working, successful New York actor, Corbin continued to act in commercials. That's when he caught the eye of the Ford Modeling Agency, one of the biggest and most famous in the world. It was quite a testament to his talents that the executives at Ford showed such interest in this little ball of fire. They signed him right away.

Corbin's cute mug began to appear regularly in newspaper and magazine print ads for major department stores like Macy's and Target and in clothing ads for Baby Gap and for Toys "R" Us. He was even the face on a toy package! There were also fashion spreads in glossy magazines like CHILD, PARENTS, and AMERICAN BABY.

The years when he was modeling professionally were the only years when Corbin *wasn't* a model student! Corbin started preschool at his neighborhood Montessori school. Precocious, bright, and

**"I was just an energetic kid. I was always happy, playful, and fun, but I had too much energy. I would get very excited. Not just in school, all the time. It got to the point where my parents couldn't even take me to restaurants."**

popular, he soon earned a reputation for being a bit *too* gregarious. He was never a bad kid—but he was also never a *quiet* kid. In Corbin's case, it had to do with his overexuberance.

He was always jumping off things—his mom's StairMaster® and open shelves—and sometimes his bouncing off the walls had painful consequences, like when he tried to hop off of the broken porch. "The steps had broken off," Corbin remembers, "so of course I felt the need to jump down from the porch all the time. I'd always get scratches and bruises. They'd heal, but I still have a scar on my nose from those days." Once, Corbin was in an airport with his parents and his grandmother, Sarah Velez. The very next day, he had a big modeling gig—he was supposed to be on the cover of a magazine. Only…he managed to jump off some stairs and hit his face! "It was only a few bruises," he says now. "But of course I never did that modeling job!"

Corbin laughs, remembering that his mother used to say if they had another child, she hoped for a girl! (She'd get that wish—three times over—in the coming years!)

*Corbin, 3, hits the stage with his dance group.*

25

*Corbin in his leather jacket—"I was a cool dresser back then!"*

*Little Corbin busts a move at his first dance recital.*

In school, Corbin even spent some time in the principal's office as a result of his big mouth. "I was constantly talking," he admits. The principal of the school assured Martha and David that they loved Corbin, but that he needed to learn the difference between his indoor voice and his outdoor voice—and that in the classroom, the indoor voice was preferred!

It is ironic that the loud voice that used to drive his teachers nuts is the same loud voice that has helped him nail a successful acting career! It's also kind of funny that when Corbin landed his very first play—at six years old—he didn't have a word to say. He played a mute! The off-Broadway production was called TINY TIM IS DEAD and was written by prolific playwright Barbara Lebow. Corbin played the nameless son of a homeless woman who tries to put on a play for Christmas but fails miserably. It was a gritty role in a sad play, and Corbin was excellent.

Corbin remembers his dad's advice. "He taught me that acting is about being natural. A lot of times people try to 'act' and it comes off as this whole dramatized thing. My dad taught me that it's more important to figure out who the character is and just to be normal."

Normal is a good way to describe Corbin's life when he wasn't posing or acting. The Reivers family spent many weekends

*Corbin dances with his cousin Jennifer at a family event.*

*Corbin performs in his first play, the off-Broadway production of TINY TIM IS DEAD. Mr. Talkative played a mute in the show.*

with his two sets of grandparents, uncles, aunts, and cousins—and there were tons, since his mom was one of seven kids. Like most families, Corbin's went on picnics and vacations, and enjoyed holiday get-togethers and weddings. Many family events were in Brooklyn, but memorably, when Corbin was three, he went with his parents to Jamaica to visit the extended Reivers brood. "It was gorgeous," Corbin recalls. "I was so little, I don't really remember everything. But I know I've got to go back."

Back home, a favorite Reivers tradition was going into New York City in early December to see the famous Christmas tree at Rockefeller Center. "I remember that so well," Corbin tells. "With the brisk weather and the snow, it's kind of magical and a lot of fun."

He loved to watch TV and read books. "I think one of the first books that I read was THE HAPPY HOCKY FAMILY. It is the funniest book. It is obviously just simple words. There's this little boy and he says, 'Do you have a red balloon? I have a red balloon.' Then it pops. Then he says, 'I have a string. Do you have a string?' Little stories like that were hilarious to me."

*Corbin, 3, on the sunny beaches of Jamaica*

Corbin has a great sense of humor; many of his earliest memories involve gales of laughter. "One time we were in a restaurant when I was around five. My dad had French fries, and he wanted to put ketchup on them. He went to pour the bottle, but nothing was coming out, so he started shaking it. Hard. Well, the top wasn't on, and suddenly, the ketchup comes flying out, going everywhere, all over us, and on the people at the next table. My dad didn't even notice! The problem is, we were so busy laughing that we couldn't stop to tell him. He was just sitting there wondering, 'What's wrong?' as he's shaking the ketchup bottle. Finally, we told him, and he had to apologize to everyone."

27

**Three-year-old Corbin in Kingston, Jamaica, his father's childhood home**

As a child, Corbin was very articulate, and could talk his way out of almost any situation. Almost…

At five years old, Corbin shows off his baseball look.

His mom's friend Mercedes recalls a day when she, Martha, David, and four-year-old Corbin went bowling. "We took Corbin," she explains, "because he was a very strong child, and Martha said, 'You have to see him bowling. He is incredible.' It was early in the evening, maybe seven o'clock. So we go to the bowling alley, and on this particular day, Corbin was not being cooperative. Let's just say he was throwing his ball in everyone else's lane. We were mortified." The bowlers in the other lanes were getting understandably angry. Finally, Martha pulled her son aside and told him something that she thought would make him behave. As Mercedes remembers it: "I was returning my bowling shoes, and I hear him screaming and crying at the top of his lungs. I turned around and asked, 'Martha, what did you do to him?' And she was just laughing. He was wailing all the way to the car and she said, 'I punished him. I told him he's not going to watch his favorite TV show for the next two days.' And I said, 'That's it? That's why he was crying like that?' In the car, he was begging her. 'Mom, will you please reconsider? Will you just stop and think about it?'"

Again, little Corbin was putting his expert negotiating skills to work. Mercedes was impressed. "I could not believe my ears. He was plea bargaining his sentence. 'Will you please reconsider? I really think this is too harsh. You really need to think about it.

Seven-year-old Corbin, with his dad and his sister Hunter.

28

THE MONTESSORI SCHOOL OF NEW YORK, INC.
EVALUATION REPORT

Corbin Relvers Reeves

Age ____ Period Sept. '92 to Jan. '93

CISES OF PRACTICAL LIFE (Aiming
environment):

uscular movements are wel
on and belongings. Need

Has a wide vocabulary with which he expresses himself
his voice a little when he talks as he is rather loud.
sounds and is learning names and letters for them. Sh

*Corbin's Montessori School evaluation confirmed
what his folks already knew: He loved to talk!*

Two days? Don't you think that's kind of harsh, Mom?' At four years old! And he fell asleep on her lap, pleading. I said, 'Martha, you're going to have to reduce the sentence.' He was so sweet, and he presented his case so well. How could you say no?"

The combination of his smarts, talent, and unbridled exuberance led his parents to put Corbin into dance class. "It was almost a natural progression for him to go into dance," Corbin's mom says. "For one thing, at the time, David was taking dance, and Corbin just loved it. He just absolutely embraced it from the beginning." He took jazz and ballet, and even though he was often the only little boy in classes full of girls, he never wanted to quit. He'd clearly inherited his mom's talent on the dance floor.

His folks didn't want him to be limited, so they also tried getting him into basketball, T-ball, and tai kwon do, though none of those really held his interest. "But dance class and acting and going with his dad on the train to his auditions— that, he loved every minute of," Martha says.

From his very earliest days, his loving parents supported him in everything he did. They set the examples for him that would put him on secure footing for his path in life—wherever that would take him. Being encouraged to pursue what he loved, coupled with life lessons and love from his parents, would take Corbin a long, long way.

*What is he asking Santa to bring?*

29

*Corbin, 5, lives it up at his cousin's wedding.*

# CALIFORNIA, HERE WE COME!

*Corbin and his new baby sister, Hunter, dress up for Halloween.*

The actors in the Reivers family were doing exceptionally well. By the mid-1990s, David had more than 100 TV commercials on his resume; he'd appeared in dozens of stage productions, as well as numerous guest-starring roles on TV shows. Corbin's young life was a hectic and joyous balance of family, modeling, TV commercials, dance lessons, school, and playtime. Best of all, the family had grown to include Corbin's sister, Hunter, who arrived when Corbin was four years old.

Still, it was becoming clearer that opportunities in New York were limited, and if both David and Corbin wanted to take their careers to the next level, a move to Los Angeles, California—the heart of showbiz—was necessary. In 1996, when Corbin was seven years old, the family packed up

*The Reivers experienced some culture shock when they moved from Brooklyn to Los Angeles. Corbin got used to it quickly—and loved riding his bike near the beach.*

On the set of the TV show BORN FREE

their Brooklyn household and headed west. Saying good-bye to grandparents, aunts, uncles, cousins, and friends, while also looking forward to new friends, neighborhoods, and acting challenges, was both scary and exciting for the close-knit clan.

Both David and Corbin experienced career boosts shortly after they settled in sunny Los Angeles. David took on bumper-to-bumper guest roles in such TV shows as BROOKLYN SOUTH, HOME IMPROVEMENT, FELICITY, and JUDGING AMY. As for Corbin, he nabbed his very first recurring role in a TV series. It was in the ABC drama HIGH INCIDENT, which was about the lives of policemen based in El Camino, California.

That same year, Corbin also booked a guest-starring role in NBC's powerhouse medical series ER. He was in the episode called "Ask Me No Questions, I'll Tell You No Lies." Although Corbin's character didn't have a name—he was referred to in the credits as "Little Boy"—the experience was totally memorable. On-screen, mega-star George Clooney gave him an injection in the rear end. Corbin got to spend time off-camera with the movie star and humanitarian, and even posed for a picture with him.

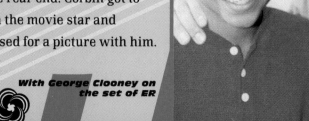

With George Clooney on the set of ER

In 1998, Corbin was cast as Matthew in an episode of the TV comedy MALCOLM & EDDIE, which starred THE COSBY SHOW's Malcolm-Jamal Warner and UNDERCOVER BROTHER Eddie Griffin. Next came small roles in big movies. At the age of nine, Corbin played Johnny in SOLDIER, a science-fiction thriller. The film starred Kurt Russell and took place in a future where select children are raised to be soldiers. "That was great," Corbin says, "but you couldn't even tell it was me in the movie because my head was shaved!" Due to violence and grittiness, SOLDIER was rated R—not exactly a movie Corbin could even go see.

On the set of SOLDIER

The next year turned out to be a huge one for Corbin; he acted in three different movies. First, he was cast as young Butch in the comedy MYSTERY MEN, with Ben Stiller, William H. Macy, and Hank Azaria. The film was about superheroes who are more "blooper" than super, yet must save the world. While MYSTERY MEN earned a friendlier PG-13 rating, it didn't last very long at the box office. That same year, 1999, Corbin appeared in the space-travel adventure GALAXY QUEST, a hilarious parody of the STAR TREK flicks. The movie won a Hugo Award for Best Dramatic Presentation and starred Tim Allen, Sigourney Weaver, and, among others, Alan Rickman, who'd go on to play Professor Snape in the HARRY POTTER movies. Corbin's character was Young Tommy Webber, a popular child actor, who was played as an adult by Daryl Mitchell.

Completing the film trifecta was a small piece called FAMILY TREE, about a young boy who must grapple both with bullies and an emotionally distant father. The boy takes a stand by protecting a beloved old oak tree from

**With his mom, Martha, on the set of GALAXY QUEST**

being cut down. Corbin played the role of Ricky, and his co-stars included Matthew and Andrew Lawrence (younger brothers of Joey Lawrence) and Naomi Judd of the famous country singing duo, The Judds.

It seems natural that Corbin and his dad would have acted together somewhere along the way, but those instances were few and far between. They appeared in a commercial for Wachovia Bank. "It was cool because we actually all played a family," Corbin recalls. "My dad, David, played the dad. My sister Hunter and I played two of his kids. It was a pretty funny commercial. The dad is sitting down on the couch when the mom comes in and says, 'Don't forget to take out the trash, honey,' and walks away. And then I walk in and my dad goes, 'Hey, son, don't forget to take out the trash.' And then I walk up to Hunter and tell her the same thing. She in turn repeats it to a younger kid—which leads to the punchline, where that kid goes into the room with the crib and tells the baby, 'Hey, you need to take out the trash.'"

*Double vision on the set of GALAXY QUEST!*

Corbin and his dad also acted together in an art house play called BABY BLUES, written by their friend, actor/director Gary LeRoi Gray. "It was a really, really fun play," Corbin recalls. "It was based on a misunderstanding—I think I've lost my sister, but really she's been with my mom the whole time. But I don't know that and search through the whole town looking for her."

*Corbin and Hunter were lucky enough to star in a commercial alongside their dad.*

*Goofing around with William H. Macy and other actors on the set of MYSTERY MEN*

| ACADEMIC ACHIEVEMENT AND EFFORT | | | | | | |
|---|---|---|---|---|---|---|
| The marks below represent an appraisal of your child's achievement and effort toward mastery of the skills and knowledge for the grade level established | ACHIEVEMENT | EFFORT | ACHIEVEMENT | EFFORT | ACHIEVEMENT | EFFORT |
| REPORTING PERIOD | 1 | | 2 | | 3 | |
| READING | | | A | A | A | A |
| WRITTEN COMPOSITION | | | A⁺ | A | A | A |
| SPELLING | | | A | A | A | A |
| HANDWRITING | | | A⁺ | A | A | A |
| ORAL LANGUAGE | | | A | A | A⁺ | A |
| MATHEMATICS | | | A | A | A | A |
| SCIENCE | | | A | A | A | A |
| SOCIAL STUDIES | | | A | A | A | A |
| HEALTH EDUCATION | | | A | A | A | A |
| MUSIC / DRAMA | | | A | A | A⁺ | A |
| ART | | | A | A | A⁺ | A |
| PHYSICAL EDUCATION | | | A | A | A | A |

EXPLANATION OF MARKS

*After filling in row after row of As, first-grade teacher Lynn Raines writes that Corbin is "every teacher's dream student."*

## The Straight-A Student

Because he was often off doing TV shows or movies, Corbin and his family had to figure out the best way for him to keep up with his schooling. His parents wanted to keep him in a normal classroom environment as much as possible. Luckily, they were able to work out a system where Corbin would be homeschooled whenever he was away acting and that he'd be doing the exact same work as his class— and it paid off. "I always got straight As," Corbin reports. He even skipped a year, going directly from sixth to eighth grade.

Confident and outgoing, Corbin makes friends easily and often; so it is no surprise that he was a popular kid in school, too. Because of his confidence and social skills, even starting school in a new state wasn't traumatic. "A lot of times when you go into a new school, it's really awkward," he concedes. "But you just have to submerge yourself into the social scene. One good thing is that if no one knows you, you can reinvent yourself— be whoever you want!"

*Corbin found inspiration in GREEN EGGS AND HAM during Carpenter Avenue Elementary School's annual Dr. Seuss Day.*

Even with his work and school schedules, he has never lost his positive attitude. He is just as fun as he's always been at home with his family. Corbin's aunt Maria Spencer, a frequent visitor to the Reivers' house, shares, "I always remember him as being outgoing. Not in an obnoxious way. He was polite, nice, and sweet. And always happy to see you."

## The Downside of the Biz

For all Corbin's successes, for all the TV and movie roles he did snare, there were many others he did not. The life of an actor—whether a child or an adult—involves constant auditions and forever being on the lookout for the next opportunity. In Los Angeles,

Corbin found himself going out on many more "calls" than he had in New York. He was older, for one thing, and for another, there were more opportunities there. But more opportunities also meant more rejection.

Rejection—those times when you're not picked—can be hard to take. Especially for a kid. Lucky for Corbin, his parents were sensitive to the process and assured him that being passed over for a role did not reflect on his talent or himself. "By the time I was seven years old, I'd been on so many auditions, I was used to it," Corbin says.

**"I understood that if I did not get the role, it wasn't that big of a deal. You just move on to the next one!"**

In his case, he was often not chosen for a particular role because he didn't match the description of the character. "A lot of times," he confides, "they weren't looking for my type." Sometimes the project calls for someone who is entirely Caucasian or entirely black. Corbin never took offense to this because it was something he had been experiencing his whole life—the reaction of other people to his racial heritage.

*Corbin relaxes at the pool*

Corbin is biracial: His mom is Italian-American, and his dad is Jamaican. When he was a kid, Corbin explained that when people met his father, they'd assume "automatically he's my dad, we look alike. People saw my mom and some automatically assumed

*Corbin and his little sister Hunter*

35

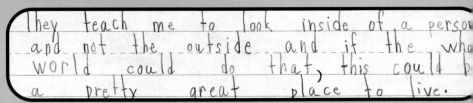

They teach me to look inside of a person and not the outside and if the whole world could do that, this could be a pretty great place to live.

*Eight-year-old Corbin wrote about being biracial and his parents' advice to him.*

that she's the nanny, second wife, girlfriend, or stepmom. Some kids came right up and asked, 'Are you adopted?' I didn't get it. It confused me. I'd ask why they thought so, and they'd say, 'Well, because your mom is white.' That's when I really started to realize that some people found that odd. But my parents always told me, look, we love each other and that's all that matters."

## Those Dancin' Feet!

The name Debbie Allen is synonymous with professional dance, choreography, and theater. The multitalented artist, who starred in the 1980s TV show FAME, is also a singer, director, producer, writer, and Emmy Award–winner several times over. The one thing she'd never done, however, was direct her own studio—that is, until the spring of 2001, when she launched Debbie Allen Dance Academy. Over 500 applicants—including Corbin—vied for the 150 spots available. Corbin was accepted immediately. The yearlong program, featuring classes in ballet, modern, jazz, hip-hop, and African dance, was intense. He had twelve dance lessons a week!

*Corbin and his family visit Winnie the Pooh while on vacation.*

Getting accepted was a feather in Corbin's cap. Excelling at the academy gave his resume a certain cachet, and the rigorous dance training no doubt helped him win the part, five years later, in HIGH SCHOOL MUSICAL.

With his career on a roll, Corbin began to experience the ups and downs of the life of a child actor in Hollywood. He counts himself incredibly lucky that his parents were by his side, helping him to interpret those experiences, and, perhaps more importantly, reassuring him that he didn't have to *stay* in the biz if he didn't want to.

**"'You can stop', they'd say, but I never wanted to. Whatever the problems were, I didn't care. I want to act."**

They reminded him that there are other people struggling in the world and that no matter what happens, he should remain thankful for his many wonderful opportunities. Acting is not about fame and fortune, but about creating work he can be proud of. Corbin takes these lessons to heart. He is humble and gracious—and continues to work just as hard on-screen as he did in school or dance class.

*Halloween fun for nine-year-old Corbin— watch out or he'll turn you into a toad!*

37

## Favorite Books

In grade school, Corbin's favorite books were

**THE TRUE STORY OF THE THREE LITTLE PIGS**

and

**THE STINKY CHEESE MAN AND OTHER FAIRLY STUPID TALES**

*Even before attending the Debbie Allen Dance Academy, Corbin could hold his own on the dance floor. Here he is with his mom at his cousin Maria's wedding.*

# SCHOOL DAZE

*At the chemistry lab of LACHSA*

When it became time for Corbin to attend high school, he wanted to follow in his mom's footsteps—that is, attend a school specializing in performing arts. "My mom always told me stories about her experiences, and I wished I could go back to New York to go where she went to school," he said. The Reivers decided to find out if there were any schools in their new hometown similar to New York's High School of Performing Arts. "We searched," Corbin says, "and found one that was *exactly* the same kind of school." They hit the jackpot with LACHSA: Los Angeles County High School for the Arts.

The school offers a full academic core curriculum—science, math, history, language arts, and foreign language—in the mornings. After lunch, arts classes begin. There are challenging programs in theater, music, dance, and visual arts. LACHSA is situated on a college campus, and best of all, since it's a public school, no tuition is charged. For these reasons, LACSHA is wildly popular. Teenagers from all over Los Angeles with an interest in the performing arts vie to attend. Each year, over 500 students apply for the ninth grade, which can only accommodate approximately forty theater students. The standards are rigorous.

*Corbin's big break: CATCH THAT KID*

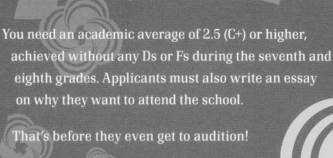

Corbin working hard

You need an academic average of 2.5 (C+) or higher, achieved without any Ds or Fs during the seventh and eighth grades. Applicants must also write an essay on why they want to attend the school.

That's before they even get to audition!

Lois Hunter, the director of Los Angeles County High School for the Arts, explains the audition process: "Aspiring theater majors have to do two contrasting monologues: something comedic and something tragic. They have to perform in front of four judges and then have an interview with me." Corbin aced all parts of the audition process and impressed Ms. Hunter during his interview. "Corbin was very, very self-motivated and self-directed," she recalls. She was especially struck by his mature and articulate response to her question: "Why are you here?"

She remembers, "Corbin immediately ran down a list. He enumerated all the things that reflected his passion. He goes to the theater. He reads plays. He does plays. His father is in the business. He's been around it and is interested in working in an ensemble. Corbin understood that theater is like sports: Unless you're standing there doing a monologue, you're interacting with others. He understood the core fundamentals of theater and why you act. He exuded confidence—I was blown away by this kid!"

So was the panel that judged Corbin's monologues.

The kid was in. Only…not for long!

As fate would have it, Corbin completed the first half of his freshman year there and then left for the best of all reasons: He got cast in a feature film! And it was the biggest role he'd ever

LACHSA
THEATRE DEPARTMENT
STUDENT OF THE YEAR
SECOND YEAR
2004
CORBIN REIVERS

A well-earned award

# Honor Roll

President's Roll 4.0 g.p.a.    Reivers, Corbin

Always a good student, Corbin was one of ten sophomores to make the President's Honor Roll.

*Corbin as technical whiz-kid Austin in CATCH THAT KID*

had in a movie. He was one of three co-stars in the teen heist film CATCH THAT KID. The movie was about a twelve-year-old girl named Maddy whose mom works for a bank. Her dad becomes ill and needs an operation, which they can't afford.

Maddy, played by Kristen Stewart, is a super athlete and rock climber. She rounds up her two best friends, tech-wiz/videographer Austin (Corbin's role) and mechanical genius Gus (played by Max Thieriot), and they use their combined skills to rob the bank where her mom works. Corbin describes his character, Austin, as "kind of a bookworm and a really computer-savvy guy. He also loves his camera."

To add a little spice to the heist, he and Gus are also rivals for Maddy's affections. During the caper, the trio must take on an ultra-modern alarm system, vicious guard dogs, and the snooping on-site security guards to even gain access the bank vault, which is suspended 100 feet in the air! Naturally, they don't exactly get away with it, but all's well that ends well in this fun film.

Corbin was beyond psyched to get the role. The only downside was the filming schedule, which conflicted with his second semester of high school. Surprisingly, the school had not faced this situation before. "Most of the kids who attend LACHSA aren't working actors yet," Corbin confides. "They get their training there and go on to perform later." While the school decided how to handle the situation, Corbin worried. "They could have just said, 'Well, bye, you're on your own. Good luck with that.'" Instead, LACHSA did something unprecedented. They worked it out so that he could stay enrolled for the rest of the first semester, and they sent him his work to complete on the set.

*Corbin celebrates his fourteenth birthday on the CATCH THAT KID set.*

40

## Why Bleu?

Bleu is actually Corbin's middle name. He chose to use it as his professional name partly to keep his career separate from his father's. His sisters also have colors for middle names. They are Hunter Gray, Phoenix Sage, and Jag Sienna.

For the second semester of his freshman year, Corbin was homeschooled and worked on the same lessons as the rest of his class. It worked beautifully. When he returned to school his sophomore year, he'd completed the same academic work as everyone else. Corbin gives major props to LACHSA for that. "They went through a lot of work and a lot of trouble to help me, which is why I love that school so much."

Academically, his favorite subjects were math and science. A self-described problem-solver, he reflects on his interests: "I love to solve problems, and math always stays the same; it's never going to change. That is, two plus two will always be four. I like the organization of math." That organization also drew him to science, and chemistry in particular.

**"What I've found is to enjoy math, you can't solely rely on what the teacher says in the classroom. You have to go home and read the textbook. When you put that together with what the teacher's explaining, it all makes a lot more sense."**

It was his sophomore year chemistry class that Corbin remembers best. His teacher, Gale Sherrodd, certainly hasn't forgotten him either. "Corbin was absolutely charming," Mr. Sherrodd tells. "Even more so, he was alert, ready to suck up knowledge. I could see it in his eyes and his face from the beginning. He would draw you to look into his eyes as you spoke. It was easy to teach with him in the class. Corbin's mind didn't wander; he was right there all the time."

The admiration runs both ways. "I did like chemistry," Corbin confirms, "especially with Mr. Sherrodd. He made it a lot of fun. He always made jokes, but he always told the *same* jokes. I loved him because he always thought he was so funny and everybody would just stand there and groan, 'Oh, Mr. Sherrodd.'"

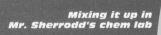

*Mixing it up in Mr. Sherrodd's chem lab*

As for Corbin's attentiveness in class, he admits it was a struggle some days. "Chemistry was my first class in the mornings, so it was early, and I'm not a morning person. There were times when I would just close my eyes and listen." Not that he was slacking off! "Mr. Sherrodd would challenge us, 'What did I just say?' And I'd repeat everything perfectly! I'd say, 'I was totally listening. I just can't actually physically open my eyes right now!'"

And what was Corbin's favorite part of science class? "I have always loved lab. I like being able to do all the different experiments and seeing what comes out of it." Of course, where there's a high school chem lab, more often than not, there's at least one disaster a semester. Corbin remembers one student setting the lab on fire but says he had nothing to do with it. Mr. Sherrodd concurs that whatever happened, Corbin wasn't involved—in fact, by the end of sophomore science, "He was my top student. He received an award for outstanding performance in chemistry, which was only given to a couple of students that year."

Corbin took another of Mr. Sherrodd's classes, an elective chemistry review class that would help him prepare for standardized tests. "Mr. Sherrodd was great! He always explained things really well. He went through each detail, and it just made sense. Sometimes, I remember, everybody would leave, and I'd stay after class and talk to him for a while. He was amazing." Corbin and his family even hung out with Mr. Sherrodd and his family once at Universal Studios CityWalk. "It was cool, you know, to see him out of his element of teaching. I find it so interesting to see teachers outside of school." Corbin jokes, "It's like they're real people, too."

Like East High in HIGH SCHOOL MUSIC, the students at LACHSA were divided into cliques. Only instead of jocks, geeks, brainiacs, and drama nerds, these groups were theater majors, music kids, dancers, and visual arts students. Corbin refused to align himself with any one group: "I like to be friends with everybody. I want to know everybody in the school, and I want everybody to know me. I like being able to

*Corbin on the set with Kristen Stewart and Max Thieriot*

just be a big happy family. When you surround yourself with a lot more people, you have backup, people that support you."

Despite the differences in the groups, the school manages to foster a "We're all in this together" spirit. As Corbin's chem teacher puts it, "At LACHSA, we're a family despite the fact that we're all different. There are visual arts students and dance students and vocalists and instrumentalists, and they all fit together in a big family. They support one another in their endeavors. They go to one another's shows. They're totally accepting."

## Almost Losing His Footing

*Corbin hits the right notes.*

The sophomore production for Corbin's year was FOOTLOOSE, based on the hit 1984 movie musical starring Kevin Bacon as Ren, a young man who moves to a small town that is so strict that pop music and dancing are not allowed. With the help of a few new friends, Ren uncovers the tragedy that led to the town's harsh rules. With his passion for song and dance, Ren turns the town around.

Naturally, Corbin wanted to audition for a part in the show—not necessarily the lead part, though. As a performer, singing wasn't where his

## Stylin'

"There was one time Corbin showed up at school, and I saw him come into the hallway with his backpack, which weighs about 300 pounds because he's got *all* his books in it, and his hair looks crazy as always, but he's wearing zebra-print pants and a matching jacket and all of his jewelry. All I could see was the zebra-print, and I just start singing the opening notes from THE LION KING as he walks in. And he just went, 'Shut up!' But he was laughing hysterically, and that will forever be burned into my eyes. That is the essence of Corbin right there. It doesn't matter what he looks like or how he's feeling, he can literally pull *anything* off."

—Classmate Whitney Ackerman

43

*"This is my glory day," enthuses Corbin about successfully tackling the role of Ren in FOOTLOOSE.*

## The Boy Who Didn't Go to His Prom

"I've been to seven proms except the one my senior year. I never got to go to my own prom—the one for my graduating class. I was working, so I wasn't with them at the time. I went to the two proms the two years before that, freshman year and sophomore year, and that was it."

confidence lay, not because he couldn't, just because he hadn't lately. "I sang in elementary school," Corbin explains. "I sang in the choir, and then my voice changed and I stopped because it was cracking and I just couldn't deal anymore." Instead, he spent the last several years honing his acting, dancing, and piano skills. He prepared a tune called "Join Us" from the play PIPPIN (partly because it "wasn't much of a strain. You don't need a huge range to do it.") The audition went wonderfully.

So when the cast list was put up for FOOTLOOSE—just like in HIGH SCHOOL MUSICAL—Corbin was shocked to find out that he'd nabbed the lead role. "I got Ren, who has to sing incredible things, like 'Almost Paradise,' which is the duet number—and he sings higher than the girl. I was freaking out—absolutely freaking out!" Corbin was flattered but had huge doubts about his ability to pull off the songs. Admitting that he's his own worst critic, he confides, "Singing has

always been something that I've been very self-conscious about."

Things got dicey when the other kids at school started to question his casting. Partly, that was due to plain old resentment. He hadn't been there for the second half of his freshman year, so a lot of people didn't know who he was. To them, he was just some new kid that appeared at the auditions and suddenly scored the lead. Lois Hunter

recalls the tough days after the cast list went up. "Some of the other kids were saying, 'How'd he get cast? He can't even sing that well.'" Worst of all, Corbin bought into their doubts and even told Ms. Hunter that he wasn't sure he could do it. "I was flabbergasted!" remembers Ms. Hunter. "Of all my students, for Corbin to say he can't do it? In the end, he had to break it down before he could build it up."

**The LACHSA program for the May 2004 production of FOOTLOOSE**

That breakdown was one of Corbin's toughest challenges. "When I'm alone, I sing all the time. It's just other people hearing me sing that makes me nervous." Obviously, singing the part of Ren would involve a lot of people hearing him!

"Singing professionally is a very, very hard thing that takes years of work, and I'm not a person that likes to take years to learn something," he admits. Not only did Corbin want to get it right away, he wanted it to be *perfect* right away!

Corbin put a lot of pressure on himself, but the pressure was not just internal. His family, friends, and teachers kept reassuring him that he had what it took to tackle the part, but in some ways, he found their faith in him even more stressful. He admits, "Everyone around me is saying, 'You're really good!' And you're sitting there going, okay, come show time, they're going to be expecting something incredible and I'm not going to be able to give it to them—and *that's* what I was freaking out about."

L.A. County H.

...SA Report Cards

| Student Name | | | Number | Grade | Sex | |
|---|---|---|---|---|---|---|
| Corbin Reivers | | | 4063 | 10 | M | 00. |

| Per | Course | Teacher | 1st Qtr | 1st Sem | 3rd Qtr | 2nd Sem | | Credit | Cit |
|---|---|---|---|---|---|---|---|---|---|
| 1 | Chemistry | Sherrodd, G | A | A | A- | A | | 5.00 | S |
| 2 | Wrld Hist/Geo | Sabnis, M | A | A+ | A | A+ | | 5.00 | O |
| 3 | Alg II | Russell, D | A | A+ | A+ | A+ | | 5.00 | S |
| 4 | Span II | Rogers,E | A | A | A+ | A | | 5.00 | O |
| 5 | Eng 10 | Behling | A | A+ | A- | A | | 5.00 | O |
| 6 | Thtr Mov Yr 2 | Gudis, E | A+ | A+ | | | | 0.00 | |
| 6-8 | Acting Yr 2 | Plumb, F | A- | A | | | | 0.00 | |
| 6-8 | Spec T Stg Comb | Lewis,D | A | A | | | | 0.00 | |
| 6-8 | Voice/Spch Yr 2 | Eick, J | A+ | | | | | 0.00 | |
| 6-8 | Rehrsl/Prodctn | Hunter, L | | | B | A | | 6.00 | O |
| 6-8 | Thtr Wrkshop | Hunter, L | | | B | A | | 3.00 | O |
| 6-8 | Theatre Techniq | Hunter, L | | | B | A | | 3.00 | O |
| 6-8 | Musical Theatre | Soerensen, G | | | A- | A | | 4.00 | S |
| 6-8 | Litr/Crit Yr 2 | Schwartz, D | A | A | | | | 0.00 | |
| 8 | Voice/Spch Yr 2 | Eick, J | | A | | | | 0.00 | |
| | Chem. Review | Sherrodd, G | A | A | | | | 0. | |
| | ...sical Theatre | Soerensen, G | | | A- | A | | | |

Corbin keeps up the good work!

45

Ms. Hunter noticed that Corbin wasn't acting like himself and asked if everything was okay. When Corbin told her what he was feeling, she told him to forget what other people were thinking. "I told him that he has a God-given gift and nobody can take that away from him. And once you start second-guessing that you have this gift, it's going to interfere with what you have to do."

His dad also stepped in. He advised, "People wouldn't tell you that you have talent, if it wasn't true. You just have to believe in it and believe in yourself more because if you don't, if you're not confident, then it's going to show in the work. You need to be fully confident in what you do."

## Rising Stress Levels

It was around that time that Corbin owned up to all the other stress that was getting in the way of his reclaiming his confidence. "I was getting straight As, and I was auditioning all the time. I was going through a lot of stuff with friends and just the whole high school thing about finding myself. There's a lot of pressure in high school, especially with the whole social factor." Trying to balance a social life with his work ethic proved harder than

*Onstage with his fellow greasers*

he would have thought. Looking back on it, Corbin remarks, "I was working so hard. A lot of times, I felt secluded because I had to go and work on what I needed to do. Not everybody was cool with that. I was only getting four or five hours of sleep every night because I got up at 5:30 to make my train to school, and I was going to bed at like 1:00 in the morning. The workload is crazy because you're working at both arts and academics. I just felt like: 'I need to breathe!'"

That's when the choreographer and director of FOOTLOOSE stepped in and urged him to do his best to concentrate and work hard for the next few months because they were sure he could handle it. Of course, Corbin agreed, but after a month, he was still struggling. Then Ms. Hunter gave him some advice that clicked. "She said, 'You have the chance to lead. You have a lot of talent, and you need to be able to talk to everybody and lift everybody up. Most of these kids have never really danced before because they're actors.'"

Those words struck a chord with Corbin, and he realized many of his fellow FOOTLOOSE cast-mates were learning dance routines for the first time. Just as he was struggling with the vocals, they were struggling with the dance moves. "I was the one who was experienced with dance. Ms. Hunter reminded me that these kids were watching me do that. I needed to step forward. It was really inspirational."

As soon as Corbin, uh, got his head in the game, he astonished everyone with his persistence. "He worked triply hard on it," attests Ms. Hunter. "His parents got him a vocal coach, but he would keep asking the musical conductor, 'Can I stay after rehearsal is over and work until I get it?' And he did. His work ethic is amazing. A lot of kids in that situation would have given up—but not Corbin."

46

Corbin modestly gives a lot of credit to his voice coach, Julia Gregory. "She took what I was confident in, dancing and acting, and she connected it to singing. So if there was something vocal that I couldn't get, if I wasn't grasping it, she'd compare it to a dance move. And then all of a sudden, I got it." The support and help of the directors, the pep talks and encouragement from Ms. Hunter, and the new kind of help from Ms. Gregory all came together for Corbin.

But one more thing ended up in the mix: Corbin's once-resentful cast-mates. Maybe it was his admission of self-doubt. Maybe it was just a matter of time, of getting to know one another. Or maybe it was his dedication, persistence, and hard work. Whatever the reason, at some point during those grueling rehearsals, even the students who questioned his casting the most, came around. They all rehearsed together and supported him in the end.

"By opening night, it was amazing. There were standing ovations, the whole thing," crows Ms Hunter. "Corbin went down to the depths, and we brought him back up. It was amazing—phenomenal, really."

## GREASE Is the Word!

Corbin's cast-mate Whitney Ackerman recalls GREASE: "At first we were disappointed in the choice. GREASE—every high school does GREASE, you know? It turned into a really fun production. Once we got into it, it became a lot more fun than it was work. We were always playing around and goofing off. We had fun developing our characters and creating little bits that we could do with each other. Corbin played Sonny, who was kind of the goofball loudmouth of the group, and I was the bully of the two. We definitely had a lot of fun… I do miss performing with him."

47

eles County High School for
*Certificate of Merit*

*Corbin Reivers*

In recognition and Appreciation for
Dedicated and Outstanding achievement in

*Chemistry*

Corbin's chemistry kudos!

But there was no rest for the weary. Just as FOOTLOOSE wound to a close, Corbin had to get to work on the next musical extravaganza, GREASE. A month later, he was back onstage at LACHSA singing and dancing with his classmates in the electrifyin' musical about the T-Birds and the Pink Ladies at Rydell High in the 1950s. But Corbin was no stranger to hard work. He played Sonny in GREASE and finished both shows to very happy audiences. He also kept up both his grades and his auditioning.

Sophomore year was Corbin's toughest, his greatest, and his most memorable school year. And…as fate would have it, his last at Los Angeles County High School for the Arts.

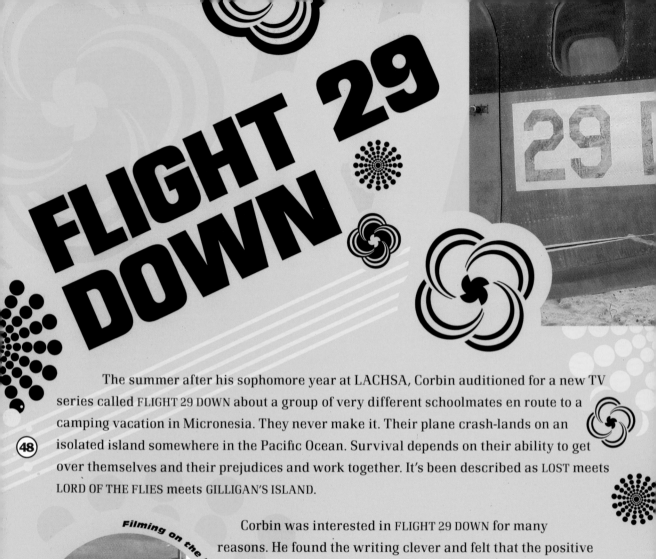

# FLIGHT 29 DOWN

The summer after his sophomore year at LACHSA, Corbin auditioned for a new TV series called FLIGHT 29 DOWN about a group of very different schoolmates en route to a camping vacation in Micronesia. They never make it. Their plane crash-lands on an isolated island somewhere in the Pacific Ocean. Survival depends on their ability to get over themselves and their prejudices and work together. It's been described as LOST meets LORD OF THE FLIES meets GILLIGAN'S ISLAND.

Filming on the beach

Corbin was interested in FLIGHT 29 DOWN for many reasons. He found the writing clever and felt that the positive message could appeal to a wide audience. The fact that it was a steady job for thirteen episodes was a major draw, too; he hadn't had a starring role in a full TV series yet.

There *was* one huge drawback, though. Accepting a role in FLIGHT 29 DOWN meant leaving school. Again. And after the trauma and eventual triumph of his sophomore year, saying good-bye was going to be doubly hard. As is typical for Corbin, he didn't make the decision lightly. He talked to his teachers. He talked to all the friends he'd made at school. He talked to his family. And, of course, he listened to his own heart.

48

Corbin in blue Hawaii
for FLIGHT 29 DOWN

That led him to…Hawaii! FLIGHT 29 DOWN would be filmed in the tropical paradise of America's fiftieth state.

Corbin had never been to Hawaii before, and he was psyched. Although he was expecting a gorgeous location, he was still stunned by the beauty of the islands. "What I always tell people about it is that you can't even imagine how beautiful it is unless you go there. The sand is like butter, and the water is so warm, so great, and so beautiful."

Originally, Corbin was called to audition for the part of Eric, a "comic relief/ instigator" character. The casting directors loved Corbin's work—only not so much in that role. They ended up calling him back for a different role, Nathan. A former boy scout who knows a thing or two about survival, Nathan wants to be the leader of the group. In fact, Nathan is a bit of a control freak, and he isn't

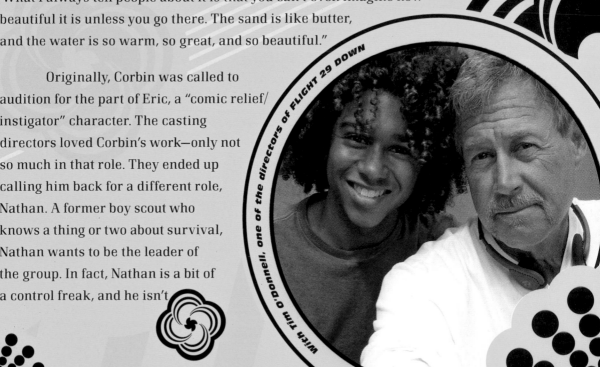

With Tim O'Donnell, one of the directors of FLIGHT 29 DOWN

much of a team player. A power struggle develops between Nathan and fellow survivor Daley (played by Hallee Hirsh), which leads to a major rivalry. What helps to make Corbin's character juicy and fun are Nathan's imperfections. Although he tries to prove to himself and to the group that he can take charge, he quickly discovers his own limitations. Throughout the season, as the group deals with one another's personalities, crushes, strengths, fears, jealousies, and insecurities, Nathan begins to understand how to work as a member of a team.

Visiting a volcano on the Big Island

## On Location

Corbin and his co-stars in FLIGHT 29 DOWN bonded super quickly!

The show was filmed on the north shore of the island of Oahu—an idyllic setting almost an hour from Hawaii's biggest city, Honolulu. Right away, Corbin and the cast fell in love with the beautiful, relaxing place that would be their home for three months. Corbin describes, "We had the beach. We had the stars at night. The island's beauty and serenity can't be imagined until you experience it yourself."

The first day of shooting was just as special as the location. Instead of beginning with Act One, Scene One, filming started with an opening ceremony and a blessing. "They brought in a holy person, almost like a priest," Corbin explains. "He blessed the set. It's a tradition when you're filming in Hawaii to have a native blessing. The whole ritual is done in Hawaiian. Holy water is poured on every crew member—it's incredible! And you sit there and you're just like wow—it's a very traditional, spiritual thing. Then, they put the leis over each of us."

*Enjoying a gorgeous sunset*

Once blessed, they were ready for action—which is exactly what they got for the next three months, on- and off-screen! Working on the show has prepared him for the worst. If Corbin ever finds himself stranded on a deserted island, he already knows how to climb a coconut tree, crack open a coconut (which is way more difficult than it sounds), and even how to start a fire with sticks. Corbin describes opening a coconut as an extremely long process. "First, you have to find a coconut on the ground or climb up the tree to get to it. Then you have to remove the husk, which is the most difficult thing to do. You have to do it in sections by getting a long, spear-type object in the ground and shoving the husk of the coconut onto the sharp part. Then you rip the husk off the shell. You have to do this several times to get all of it off. Then you take the blunt end of something such as a knife and hit the coconut around the center until it cracks open. When you open it up, you have to do it carefully so as not to spill the milk inside because that's the best part. I kept the shell of the first coconut I ever opened."

Behind the scenes of
FLIGHT 29 DOWN

What about igniting a fire without matches? "Starting a fire with sticks just takes a lot of energy out of you," Corbin reports. "It really is a workout because your arms get so tired from moving that stick back and forth."

Corbin and the other actors got to film some extra-cool shots. In a huge storm scene, they had to endure the chaos of having water constantly poured over them, and then there was the infamous pig episode, where he and another character ran through the jungle trying to catch a pig. The off-camera pig adventures were even more ridiculous. The pig actually got away! Watching the entire crew of twenty grown men chasing a pig up and down a mountain was one of the funniest things the cast had ever seen.

51

Hallee Hirsh, Corbin, Allen Alvarado, and
Kristy Wu relax between takes.

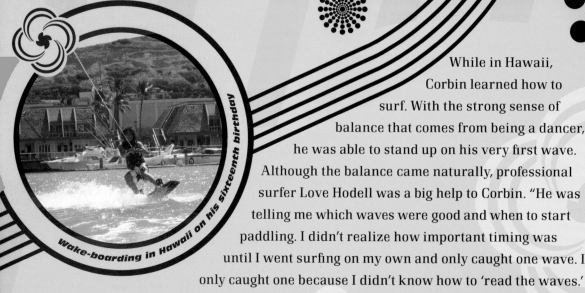

Wake-boarding in Hawaii on his sixteenth birthday

While in Hawaii, Corbin learned how to surf. With the strong sense of balance that comes from being a dancer, he was able to stand up on his very first wave. Although the balance came naturally, professional surfer Love Hodell was a big help to Corbin. "He was telling me which waves were good and when to start paddling. I didn't realize how important timing was until I went surfing on my own and only caught one wave. I only caught one because I didn't know how to 'read the waves.' That's the real hard part to surfing. It is not so much the action of standing up on the board as much as knowing *when* to stand up on the board. It's something I'm still learning how to do."

Best of all, Corbin grew to really understand his character and got to portray Nathan's journey from stubborn wannabe leader to the real deal.

On- and off-camera, Corbin made some of the best friends he's ever had.

## "The cast was amazing. We got along so well from the day we met— we clicked right away."

Find out what Corbin has to say about his much-loved co-stars.

### Hallee Hirsh

Hallee Hirsh played Daley, the girl who competed with Nathan to be the group leader. "Oh, man, I miss Hallee. She's the sweet one. Hallee's so cool, and the one closest in age to me, so we did school together. Since we weren't in an actual classroom, she was kind of my link to the outside world. She's offbeat in the way she dresses and the kind of music she listens to— she says she was born in the wrong era. She should have lived in the 1920s and 1930s."

*Kristy, Corbin, Hallee, and Allen on the set*

## Lauren Storm and Jeremy Kissner

Lauren Storm and Jeremy Kissner play Taylor and Eric. "They are so funny together!" Corbin says, "They make the greatest team. In real life, Lauren is always very caring.

### He's My Friend!

"Corbin...that boy has been such a good friend to me. He's so kind and giving of himself...He's young— there's this part of him like, 'Everything is fun! Everything is new! Let's see a movie! Let's play! Let's go bowling!' But at the same time, he's got a really old soul and gets what really matters in life, like being a good person to everybody, working hard, remembering your family, remembering where you came from. He's got that moral base that many kids don't have, that many successful people don't learn until later on in life."

—Lauren Storm

Lauren knows everybody in the business—she's become my networking friend, the one who introduces me to everybody. She's just been great. She's the person that I see the most out of all of them because we have the same publicist and we go to events together all the time.

"Jeremy was the one who always made me laugh, the funny one. He just knows all these random facts about high school chemistry and the periodic table of the elements, about how to take care of random animals...Stuff that makes you go, 'Why do you even know that?' And you never know what he's going to do. Once we were all sitting around watching TV, and he balled up a piece of paper and just threw it in Holly's mouth. He's very smart. I found him fascinating, and I loved hanging out with him."

Corbin and Jeremy out for sushi

*The cast of FLIGHT 29 DOWN on the town*

## Kristy Wu

"Kristy Wu played Melissa. Kristy was the one that I confided in the most—I talked to her about everything. Whatever was going on, especially relationship-wise, she was the one I talked things over with, and she did the same with me. She's nothing like her character. She has the combat boots on and she's hard-core—in a cool way."

## Johnny Pacar

Johnny Pacar played Jackson, the kid who was new to the school, and was, at first, standoffish and secretive. "Johnny, we love Johnny. We call Johnny 'Mister Cool.' He has this way of talking—he's very soft spoken. In the first season, he had this mystery thing about him, but in the second season, we hung out and grew close as friends—he became like a brother to me."

## Allen Alvarado

Allen Alvarado played the tagalong little brother, Lex. "He was like our little brother off-camera, too. It was funny because his parents were there, and they

*Corbin and Allen meet a Komodo dragon.*

were so young, they seemed closer to our age! Allen is really smart, really incredible. If anyone ever accidentally cursed on the set in front of him, you had to pay a fine of a dollar. I try not to curse anyway, so it was not a problem for me!"

## Behind the Scenes–The Upside...

Life behind the scenes of FLIGHT 29 DOWN was just as full and crazy as in the show. There was a major fun-factor upside, which can also be seen as a downside as well. For three months, the entire cast was together 24/7! In a very isolated area!

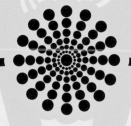

## Practical Jokes on the Set

"Lauren can sleep through just about anything, and she falls asleep a lot on set. So one day, when she was sleeping in her chair, we took a whole bunch of candy wrappers, water bottle labels, and basically any trash we could get our hands on and stuck them to her. Then we snapped some pictures and pulled the wrappers off of her before she woke up. Later that day, we showed her the pictures and she just hung her mouth open and burst out laughing. The best part was that the next day, she feel asleep again.

Another similar prank occurred the second season, only this time it was to me. I fell asleep in my chair and because the scene had finished, they were moving the set. Well, they moved everything away and left me sitting there. Then they took some shrubbery and placed it around my chair. When I woke up, I was in this plant jungle all by myself. I finally got out of it and everyone was standing there laughing. It was hysterical."

They all lived together in one big condo unit. While it was just two blocks from the beach where the show was shot, it was pretty much in the middle of nowhere. And it was just a three-story building—not a hotel. There was no room service, no lobby. The twelve-room pad was spacious enough so that everyone had his or her own room. "You come out your door, walk three feet, and go into the next person's room," Corbin describes. "It was so cool because there was nobody else there. We ruled that place, and we were at each other's places all the time! We hung out, we watched movies, and at night, we'd go up to the patio roof to watch the sunset and the stars." When they ventured out of the condo on their days off, the young cast sometimes went snorkeling, swimming, and surfing. In their time together, they even developed their own traditions. They ate at the restaurant Bonzai Sushi at least once a week—sometimes ending up there three times in one week. And they developed an obsession for the game Boggle® and could often be found playing between scenes or over lunch.

*Corbin doing one of his own stunts*

### ...And the Downside!

Could this dream scenario even have a downside? It depends on what the actors needed at any given moment. They were far from shops, clubs, movie theaters, and a selection of restaurants. Rental cars were pricey—and even when they all splurged for one, Honolulu was more than forty-five minutes away. In other words, like their characters, they were far from civilization—for ten and a half weeks. Corbin concedes, "We saw each other every day at work, then we'd come home and hang out after work. One reason we got so close is because we didn't have anything else to do!" They made the best of it, though. Without any neighbors to complain, they turned up the music in the rooms and hosted their own dance parties!

56

Corbin missed his family, too. He was used to being in a big, bustling household with his three sisters and his parents. Being without them was a downer. Not that he was completely deprived of his relatives. Showbiz law insists that anyone under the age of eighteen must have a parent or guardian on the set with them at all times. Because his parents couldn't get away for three straight months, his extended family happily pitched in. For one month, Corbin's aunt Maria Spencer (one of his mom's sisters) was there with him—she treated him to a parasailing ride in Honolulu for his sixteenth birthday. For another month, his dad came out. For fun, they hopped over to the Big Island of Hawaii where they took a small plane over a volcano! For the third month, Corbin's mom came to keep him company. The different family members and the outings they took helped to relieve Corbin of some of the boredom that came with being in such an isolated spot for so long.

**The cast of FLIGHT 29 DOWN the morning of its premiere**

*"There's an area on the Big Island of Hawaii where people go and they write messages with white rocks on the black lava landscape," recalls Corbin. "When my dad and I were over there during the first season of filming FLIGHT 29 DOWN, we wrote 29 DWN with the rocks. The second season, Lauren went back there and saw that it was still there."*

## …And the School Side!

It wasn't all filming and fun 'n' games, at least not for Corbin and Hallee, the two cast members in high school. Since FLIGHT 29 DOWN was filmed between January and March, they had to fit their studies in as if they were in a regular classroom. Corbin explains it, "The law says we have to get in at least three hours of school each day while we're filming. We worked with a tutor, but it was difficult at times. We might start on a subject, do five minutes of work, then get called to the set for filming!" After a particular scene would be shot, Corbin would go right back to his tutor. But often, "No sooner do we get settled back in, then they call us back to the set again! It got annoying at times, but I love what I do so much that somehow it all got accomplished."

## …And the Real Side

FLIGHT 29 DOWN debuted October 1, 2005 as part of Discovery Kids™ on NBC and aired on Saturdays for the first season. Corbin took away an important message from it: "Whatever situation you're put into, you can get through it. You never know where life will take you. Prepare for anything, because you never know what can happen. It's survival, whether you're lost in the woods, or trapped by a hurricane. It's all about working together as a team to try and survive." Speaking of working together as a team… that message was never clearer than in Corbin's next big hit!

## Corbin Sings!

Remember those voice lessons Corbin took to tune up for FOOTLOOSE? They started paying extra dividends sooner than expected. "I did a song," Corbin reveals. "For FLIGHT 29 DOWN, I recorded this song called 'Circles,' which was played as background music in the episode when my character's going through this thing where he likes this girl and doesn't know how to tell her. That was my first time in the recording studio, and it just turned out great." And that's what led to a recording contract! More on that on page 94!

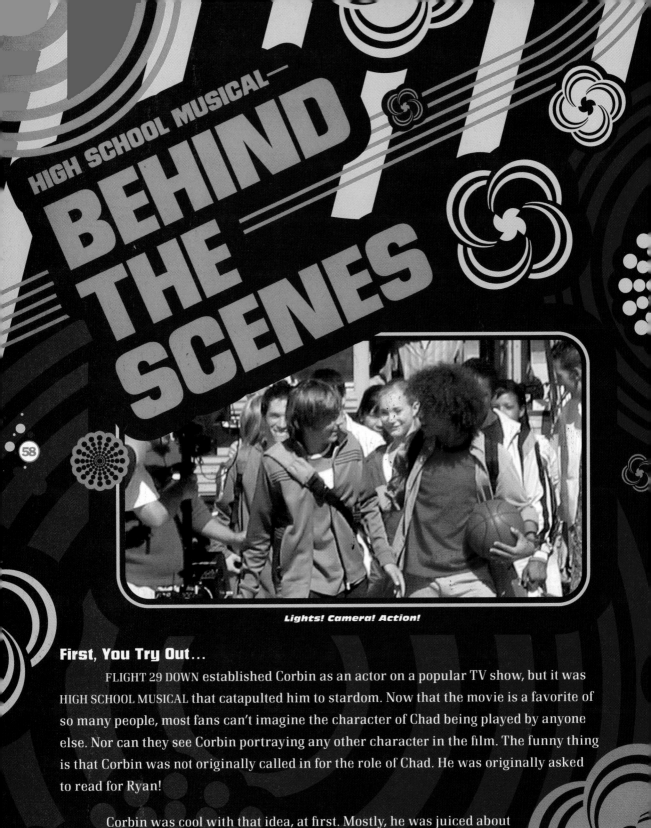

# HIGH SCHOOL MUSICAL— BEHIND THE SCENES

*Lights! Camera! Action!*

## First, You Try Out...

FLIGHT 29 DOWN established Corbin as an actor on a popular TV show, but it was HIGH SCHOOL MUSICAL that catapulted him to stardom. Now that the movie is a favorite of so many people, most fans can't imagine the character of Chad being played by anyone else. Nor can they see Corbin portraying any other character in the film. The funny thing is that Corbin was not originally called in for the role of Chad. He was originally asked to read for Ryan!

Corbin was cool with that idea, at first. Mostly, he was juiced about being in the movie. Why did he want to be in it?

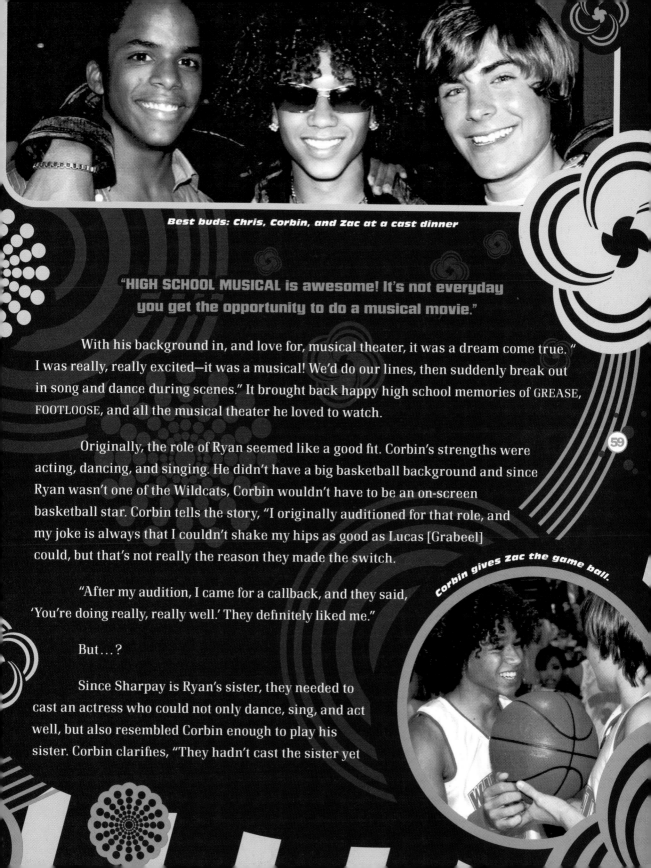

Best buds: Chris, Corbin, and Zac at a cast dinner

**"HIGH SCHOOL MUSICAL is awesome! It's not everyday you get the opportunity to do a musical movie."**

With his background in, and love for, musical theater, it was a dream come true. "I was really, really excited—it was a musical! We'd do our lines, then suddenly break out in song and dance during scenes." It brought back happy high school memories of GREASE, FOOTLOOSE, and all the musical theater he loved to watch.

Originally, the role of Ryan seemed like a good fit. Corbin's strengths were acting, dancing, and singing. He didn't have a big basketball background and since Ryan wasn't one of the Wildcats, Corbin wouldn't have to be an on-screen basketball star. Corbin tells the story, "I originally auditioned for that role, and my joke is always that I couldn't shake my hips as good as Lucas [Grabeel] could, but that's not really the reason they made the switch.

"After my audition, I came for a callback, and they said, 'You're doing really, really well.' They definitely liked me."

But…?

Since Sharpay is Ryan's sister, they needed to cast an actress who could not only dance, sing, and act well, but also resembled Corbin enough to play his sister. Corbin clarifies, "They hadn't cast the sister yet

Corbin gives Zac the game ball.

59

Corbin's agents Brandy Gold (left) and Bonnie Liedtke (right) visited Corbin on the HSM set.

Bonnie remembers that during the visit, "All he could do was thank me for the job that he had earned. He worked so hard and rightfully earned it." Looking back, she recalls meeting Corbin shortly after he arrived in California. "He was an adorable little boy who was a triple threat! What more could you ask for? He could sing, dance, and act! He was also one of the cutest, sweetest young boys you could ever find. Throw in a great set of parents, and it was a home run for myself and the company!" She sees bright things in the future—and she's not the only one! "I will pray that I continue to be his agent for a very long time. I enjoy working with actors of his caliber. He makes me rise to the occasion."

and were having a hard time finding a match." Instead of expanding the search, the casting directors did a U-turn and offered Ashley Tisdale and Lucas Grabeel roles as the Evans siblings. But the producers and casting directors weren't about to cut Corbin loose!

## And Then, You Try Out Again— for Another Role!

"They still wanted me," Corbin says, "so I read for Chad. Chad is a very off-the-wall character. He is hyper and crazy, so he is always bouncing around. And he is very much into basketball." The audition went incredibly well. "I made them all laugh. So, in the end, they liked me even better in that role. It was my first time being cast as a comic relief character. I'm the serious guy in FLIGHT 29 DOWN, and I was the dorky computer nerd guy in CATCH THAT KID. Chad was the first time that I really got to be the cool, crazy, comic relief, which was really fun!"

Although the casting process was a huge success for Corbin, he admits that it was extremely nerve-racking. Because he auditioned for more than one role and because HIGH SCHOOL MUSICAL required acting, singing, and dancing talent, there were many components to the tryouts, and the process went on for a long time. "I went in, I changed roles. Then I went in for a callback. Then I had to go in again and sing. And then they said, OK, you're doing great. Now, we need you to meet the director. I remember that first time I walked in the room to meet him. I was actually kind of nervous, even though I don't usually get nervous."

He was able to get past his anxieties and perform both the song and the dance he had prepared for director Kenny Ortega. "Finally, they needed to see if I could handle the basketball—so it was really like a multi-part test. OK, you passed this part, but there's still another part."

Playing basketball, of course, was where it got a little dicey. Although he had a hoop in his backyard, Corbin hadn't played that much b-ball. Luckily, the powers-that-be were impressed by Corbin's other talents and had faith that he could pick it up.

Corbin was at his agent's office when the call came in that he'd snagged the role. "They said, 'You got it!' And I just started yelling. I was so happy." His joy was dimmed only slightly when he realized how quickly he'd have to start filming. He got the magic call on a Friday and the following Monday, he had to fly out to...Utah.

*Practicing his b-ball moves*

Yep, Salt Lake City, Utah, played the part of Albuquerque, New Mexico, where HIGH SCHOOL MUSICAL takes place.

## Who's Who in the Cast

Troy Bolton . . . . . . . . . . . .ZAC EFRON
Chad Danforth . . . . . . . .CORBIN BLEU
Gabriella Montez . . .VANESSA ANNE HUDGENS
Sharpay Evans . . . . . . . . ASHLEY TISDALE
Jason Cross . . . . . . . . . RYNE SANBORN
Ryan Evans . . . . . . . . .LUCAS GRABEEL
Taylor . . . . . . . . . .MONIQUE COLEMAN
Kelsi . . . . . . . . . . . .OLESYA RULIN
Zeke . . . . . . .CHRISTOPHER WARREN JR.
Mrs. Darbus . . . . . . . . .ALYSON REED
Coach Bolton . . . . . . . .BART JOHNSON

### The Cast Bonds

Before getting cast as Chad, Corbin had only met one of his other cast-mates; during the audition process, he did a scene with Monique Coleman (Taylor), but that was it.

*Corbin and Ashley get ready for the Expedition Everest ride at Disney. "It's a great ride. Ashley and I had so much fun."*

The cast of HIGH SCHOOL MUSICAL party at a restaurant called the Crab Shack near the set. The cast just got up and taught the other diners the HSM dance steps!

And he wasn't sure anyone really knew, before getting to Utah, exactly what they were in for. Some of the cast members hadn't realized the extent of the music and dance in the film. But, after the first two days in Utah, Corbin says, "Everyone realized what it was."

In a scenario that was similar to Corbin's experience with FLIGHT 29 DOWN, the entire cast bunked together—this time, not in a condo, but in the Little America Hotel in Salt Lake City.

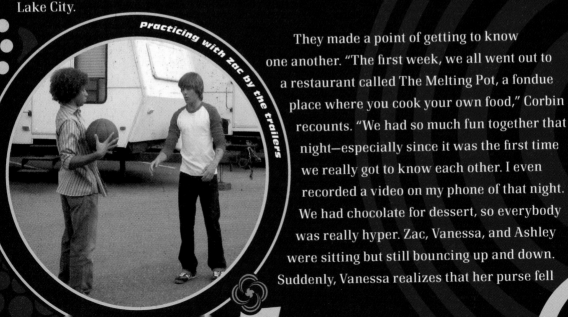

practicing with Zac by the trailers

They made a point of getting to know one another. "The first week, we all went out to a restaurant called The Melting Pot, a fondue place where you cook your own food," Corbin recounts. "We had so much fun together that night—especially since it was the first time we really got to know each other. I even recorded a video on my phone of that night. We had chocolate for dessert, so everybody was really hyper. Zac, Vanessa, and Ashley were sitting but still bouncing up and down. Suddenly, Vanessa realizes that her purse fell

## !!!Danger Zone!!!

As the cast came together as a true family, they pulled practical jokes on one another. Corbin's favorite is the one Zac played on him. "The bathroom in my trailer had been going haywire," recalls Corbin. "One morning, we walked in, and it smelled like sulfur. There was something messing up the pipes. I left, but apparently Zac stayed. When I came back, there was all this yellow crime scene tape all over my trailer and orange cones placed around it. The caution tape was even over the front door so I couldn't get in. For a minute, I panicked, thinking, all my stuff is in there, and I can't get in! What is going on? How am I going to get my stuff? I was afraid to open the door. And then I turned around and there was Zac with his camera! He called it the Danger Zone!"

down—everyone's bouncing up and down and her purse just falls." They ended up howling with laughter as everything spilled out of her bag. In silly moments like these, the cast discovered right away that they were going to have a lot of fun filming HIGH SCHOOL MUSICAL. Now, whenever they get together, Corbin pulls out his phone and they all watch the video of that night at The Melting Pot.

"A couple of weeks later, we came back to the hotel after dinner and it was late, probably like 11:30. It'd been a great day, a great dinner. We had just learned a new dance that day. Rehearsals had gone well, so our energy was still pumped. It was almost like in the movie and we said, 'Let's do the dance!' We all lined up in the middle of the lobby of the hotel and start doing 'We're All In This Together.' The other guests who happened to be in the lobby must have been scratching their heads going, 'What are these kids doing?' I'm sure we caused a commotion, but we were all really just energetic and excited."

Once they got to know one another, the cast would take outings every weekend to the Gateway, a mall in downtown Salt Lake City. They would go shopping, enjoy the restaurants, and catch movies there. There was one movie in particular that the cast loved to watch. "We became obsessed with ANCHORMAN when we were shooting HSM. It's a very funny movie, and Will Ferrell is hilarious. We would constantly quote the movie." To top it off, there is a side-splitting scene where comedy greats Will Ferrell, Paul Rudd, David Koechner, and Steve Carrell all sing a song together in the film, and the cast loved it. Corbin shares, "'Afternoon Delight' became one of our favorite songs and we would sing it all the time. There is actually an outtake of me and the guys singing it while shooting the reconciliation scene on the roof."

## Corbin Dishes on His Co-Stars

### Zac Efron:

"Zac is one of the nicest guys I've ever met. What I like about Zac is that he's always been a very respectful person, and now that he's on the cover of every single magazine—a huge star—he's stayed humble. He is very supportive of me and says 'You're going to be really great,' 'You're going to go far,' and things like that. I'm just like whoa, that's awesome. He's just a really cool guy—a really respectful guy."

### Ashley Tisdale:

"I love Ashley. She knows this business so well. She's always aware of what's going on. She knows that people are watching her and in interviews, she's articulate and very professional. I admire that! "

### Vanessa Anne Hudgens:

"Vanessa's really, really fun. She's thoughtful and she's always been nice to me. At the same time, she's really cool. She's a total party."

### Lucas Grabeel:

"Lucas is the funny one. He's an artistic guy—a musician. What I like about Lucas is his respect for himself and his love for what he does, he's really passionate."

*Corbin and Vanessa mug for the camera.*

## Monique Coleman:

"Monique. I love that girl to death. She's just such a sweetheart. Every single time we see each other, it's nothing but huge hugs. She's a beautiful girl, but she's very down-to-earth and totally not into superficial vanity. She's very caring and giving and loving."

## Rehearsals: Getting Their Heads— and Feet—in the Game!

Of course, it wasn't all goofing around, dinners out on the town, and breaking into song in the lobby—they had a movie to shoot. Before filming got under way, there were rehearsals. When Corbin and the cast describe the rehearsals, the word "grueling" comes up a lot! Or, let's say, "suffering for their art."

*Monique and Corbin riding Expedition Everest*

65

*Ryne's friends visit the guys on the set.*

*The cast does an interview with ACCESS HOLLYWOOD at Walt Disney World's Expedition Everest opening.*

HIGH SCHOOL MUSICAL was on a tight schedule—after two intense weeks of rehearsal, they had just over twenty-eight days to get the entire movie shot—and that includes rehearsal time! That translated into dancing, singing, and basketball rehearsals for eight hours a day. "It was like boot camp," says Corbin. "Up at 6 AM, breakfast at 6:30, on the set by seven. And for the next eight hours, we were all about learning the routines."

Which cast member was always on time? Corbin gives Lucas props for always being ready to go. "He was always the first one downstairs waiting for everyone else." As for the one who took the longest to leave the house, Corbin gives himself that award. He was on time to the set, but he definitely took the longest to get ready. "I take forever to fix my hair," he admits.

Once on the set, they would get right down to business, rehearsing and learning the dances. With Corbin's dance training, he picked up the dances quicker than anybody. Zac, on the other hand, admits to being a slower learner in the dance department. "When he first started, he was definitely having a little

## Where did the cast hang out when they weren't working?

"Most of the time," Corbin reports, "we liked to hang out in the school at the cafeteria where 'Status Quo' was filmed."

66

trouble," Corbin remembers. "But I am very impressed at how hard he worked to give the amazing result that he did." While preparing for the energetic dance numbers, some cast members sustained minor injuries. Zac told SCHOLASTIC MAGAZINE that at times he was so sore he couldn't believe he could walk! "I had so many muscle pulls and shin splints. It took a lot of Gatorade and aspirin to get me through dancing and basketball rehearsals. But I learned more in those two weeks than I'd learned in the previous years. Every second was worth it."

Corbin and Chris do their impression of Ryan and Sharpay.

In the same interview, Ashley added, "Our bodies hurt so much. We were so sore, but it was great. It was such great exercise."

Corbin breaks down the way the song and dance rehearsals worked: "'Stick to the Status Quo' was the first musical number we did during rehearsals. That was the first time we all performed together. It was a two-day shoot, and it's funny because in the first take we did, we were full of crazy energy, but it was extremely unorganized. Everybody was running around, and we forgot everything. As we did more takes, it just got better and better and better."

**"That was the first time that all of us realized 'Wow, we're going to do this. This is going to be good. This is going to be REALLY good.'"**

Chris Warren Jr. plays Zeke, the jock in search of the best crème brûlée recipe. His favorite scene, with Ashley Tisdale, came after the credits. "She says that she likes my cookies and then tackles me and I make her some crème brûlée. That scene was written, but we didn't think that we were going to do it. It barely made the cut." For him, the scene was bittersweet. "It was Ashley's last scene before she went back to California. It was close to the end of the day, and so we had to hurry and get it done and we did."

One of Chris's best memories of hanging out with Corbin was when Corbin showed him all of the songs and dances of THE ROCKY HORROR PICTURE SHOW in his trailer. "He was just showing it to me because I had never seen it. And he was showing it to me and showing me all the moves and stuff. He knew every move. He can do the whole show." Another time, the two actors and their parents all went out to dinner and had a great time. Spending time away from the group was cool and allowed them to get to know each other better. "We were there for about three hours having a really deep conversation," Chris remembers.

From the basketball player with a passion for baking to the cello-playing skater dude, the characters in "Stick to the Status Quo" are a lot of fun. Fans all have their favorites. For Corbin, "Out of the people who admit what they like to do, I like the brainiac whose passion is hip-hop. She did such a great job with that part. It's hilarious. But one of my other favorite parts in that song is when Sharpay is singing and Ryan tries to sing as well, but she puts her hand up to him and stops him. I still crack up every time I see that."

The next number the cast tackled was "Get'cha Head in the Game." Only the guys appeared in that piece. "For me, that was the toughest one," Corbin admits, "because that meant dealing with the basketball—and I had to do a lot." The b-ball moves were the most worrisome part of it all for him. Dancing, acting, and singing were all, as he puts it, in his "comfort zone." Basketball? Not so much. He candidly admits, "I was the worst out of everybody at basketball. I was the one who accidentally sent the ball flying everywhere. We had multiple takes of that one—and meanwhile, I'm getting so mad at myself. Everybody else reassured me, saying, 'Calm down; it's okay, everybody's balls are flying everywhere,' but it is happening to me on every take!"

Practice makes perfect!

69

The situation was not so different than when he was back in school, struggling with the singing for FOOTLOOSE. Then, as with HIGH SCHOOL MUSICAL, Corbin's credo remained the same: "I need to get this done, and it's going to happen." And Corbin made it happen.

"I learned how to spin a basketball. I got really good at it. I was starting to do tricks like switching fingers, spinning on my elbow, and all this really cool stuff. I just became obsessed with it."

## The Grand Finale

The hardest sequence for the whole cast to nail was the last song, "We're All in this Together," because there were just so many people onstage at the same time. Over 400 Utah locals had been hired as extras, and many of them appeared as background dancers in that final number. "We were bumping into each other," Corbin says. "We just couldn't seem to get a perfect take," until director/choreographer Kenny Ortega had an idea. He called everyone onstage together and told them to think about…Tokyo. Corbin chuckles remembering, "Tokyo? We

70

*Rockin' out at the Rocking Roller Coaster*

*Corbin joins his sisters, Hunter, Phoenix, and Jag, on Disney's Aladdin Magic Carpet ride. "Everybody recognized me," he laughs. "The Magic Carpet is a little kid's ride, and I had to go on it because the girls wanted me to take them on it….I was just sitting there, like, 'I swear I'm here with my little sisters, I'm not riding this ride for me!'"*

Corbin, Ryne, and Chris practice their camera-ready faces.

They are serious one minute and all smiles the next.

asked, 'What's a city in Japan got to do with this song and dance?' And Kenny put it to us this way, 'Right now, you guys are dancing like you're at a club and you're just having fun. I don't want it to be like that. I need this to be like Tokyo.' We all stand there, thinking, 'What?'"

Kenny went on to explain that in Tokyo there are so many people in such close proximity that they learn to be observant and understanding of their surroundings. Corbin recalls, "He told us that in Tokyo, there are millions of people, and it's ridiculous how many people walk the streets all the time. It's just like floods and floods of people. But they all walk, and nobody bumps into each other. Everybody's aware of their surroundings, and they weave in and out, like this whole fluid motion. That is how he needed us to dance."

When the maestro started to demonstrate, Corbin and his cast-mates were in awe. "That was so helpful! He has a vision, and he explains it so well, and you realize, wow, that makes complete sense. And you know what? The next time we did it, everybody felt it. Everybody got it. It was no longer just us dancing, it was us sensing each person nearby, and having this connection, and actually feeling the heat and the energy of the person next to you or behind you. When we finished the dance, we'd gotten it perfectly. That was something, the way he was able to bring things out of us. It was just incredible."

71

East Side & Queens

F Queens To Jamaica all times

57 Street

Lucas and his sister, and Monique, Zac, and Corbin, hop on the F train in New York City.

Corbin admits that he always gets a little jittery before live performances, like the one the cast did for the TODAY show. "But once I get into the performance, my adrenaline gets going and my nerves just vanish." Filming a movie is different, since the actors know that there will be several takes of each scene or dance number. The final number was one exception to the rule. "I think the one time that everyone probably felt the same nervousness was during the final number. Kenny Ortega told us that they were going to set off balloons and confetti cannons during one of the takes, but he didn't tell us which take because he wanted real, genuine reactions. We only had one shot to get it right, so

## THE TEEN CHOICE AWARDS

HIGH SCHOOL MUSICAL cleaned up at the 2006 TEEN CHOICE AWARDS. On Sunday, August 20th, they took home the award for CHOICE TV SHOW (Musical or Comedy). Zac Efron was crowned TV CHOICE BREAKOUT STAR and he and Vanessa Anne Hudgens took home the prize for CHOICE CHEMISTRY for their portrayals of misunderstood lovebirds Troy and Gabriella. After the awards, Corbin said, "The coolest part about TEEN CHOICE AWARDS was the amount of incredible performers that we were surrounded by. To be honored with an award presented by Ne-Yo, JoJo, and Kristin Cavallari was such a fulfilling achievement." To make an already exciting evening more memorable, Corbin got to spend some time in the same place as one of his idols. "For me, Johnny Depp is someone that I look up to. Unfortunately, I wasn't able to see him because we had already accepted our award and had to go backstage, but the fact that I was receiving an award at the same event that he was means a lot to me."

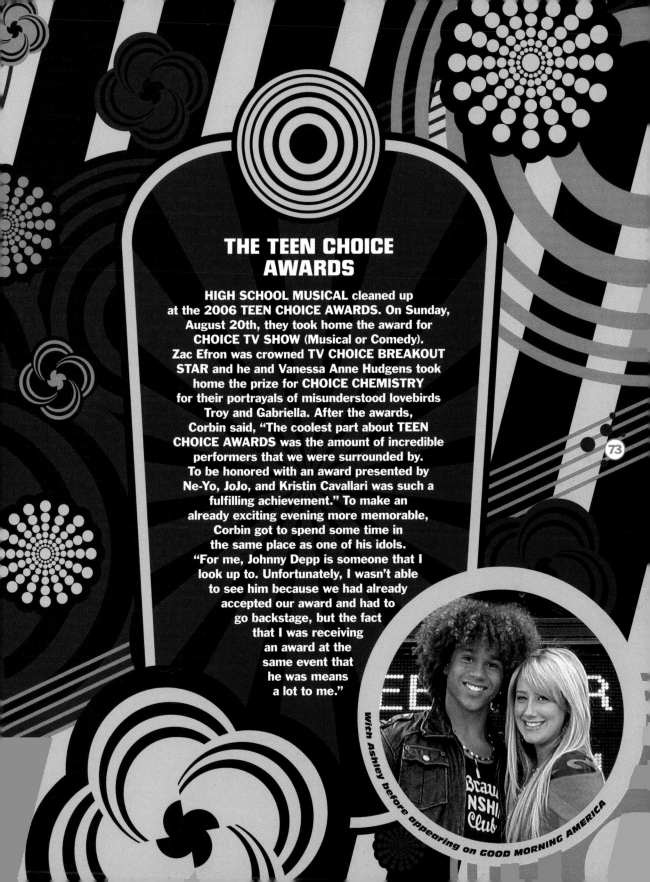

With Ashley before appearing on GOOD MORNING AMERICA

73

we were all extremely worried about messing up on that take. In the end, we all put out our best performance during that take. It was awesome!"

## Corbin's Favorite Scenes

Beyond the dance numbers, the acting scenes Corbin had with Zac were his favorites. He explains, "The thing about Chad and Troy is that they've known each other since kindergarten; they didn't just meet in high school. So the goal was to make Chad as comfortable as possible around Troy—he'd do things like put Troy in a little headlock and give him a nuggie. I wanted them to come off as relaxed and comfortable as possible, because to Chad, Troy is family."

*Corbin in the hot seat in the makeup trailer.*

The scene that ranks No. 1 with Corbin is when Chad is trying to convince Troy not to go to callbacks and not to be in the musical. In this scene, the audience gets to see the mischievous side of Chad. At first, Chad just pleads with his friend. But then he takes matters to a new level and tries to sabotage Troy's budding relationship with Gabriella. Best buds or not, Chad tricks Troy into saying things about Gabriella—things that she will see on video. "I'm in the trophy room," Corbin explains, "and I'm telling him about all these past players that would do great things—laying the guilt on—and that was the first time that I actually got to be a little bit of a bad guy."

Corbin's character, Chad, and Monique's character, Taylor, team up to try to prevent Troy and Gabriella from getting together and from scoring the leads in the upcoming musical. Corbin found it particularly interesting to have the opportunity to portray the antagonist in a story. He'd always played a good guy before, "but in that scene, I felt so sneaky." And it was fun!

Corbin wonders if he'll ever get another chance to play a bad guy—or another good guy who does a bad thing—because "I don't think I'm a mean or evil-looking person."

*Corbin and Ashley are joined by Aly and A.J. Michalka during the Expedition Everest opening party. "They closed the whole park," Corbin recalls. "It was awesome. We could go on the rides as many times as we wanted."*

Another of his favorite scenes with Zac was the library scene, when Nathan tells Troy about the picture in his mom's refrigerator. "I flubbed my line," Corbin remembers. "I was supposed to say 'My mom,' but I got tongue-tied and started stuttering." Corbin and Zac burst into laughter. "It was so hard for me to keep a straight face in every take after that."

## The Last Day…or Was It?

The cast reunites at Walt Disney World.

The cast shared countless laughs together. They had a lot of fun and learned a lot from one another and from Kenny Ortega. So the final day on the set of HIGH SCHOOL MUSICAL was bittersweet for the cast members. The rehearsals, the filming, the dinners, the practical jokes, and the times they spent together were very special, so it was hard to say good-bye. They knew, of course, they would see each other again, most likely at the premiere of HIGH SCHOOL MUSICAL, but they had *no idea* just how much they would be together in the near future.

75

## THE EMMY AWARDS

HSM garnered more Emmy nods than any other show in the history of the Disney Channel! They won for:

**OUTSTANDING CHILDREN'S PROGRAM**

**OUTSTANDING CHOREOGRAPHY FOR A MINISERIES, MOVIE, OR SPECIAL**

They were also nominated for:

**OUTSTANDING CASTING FOR A MINISERIES, MOVIE, OR SPECIAL**

**OUTSTANDING MUSIC AND LYRICS FOR "BREAKING FREE"**

**OUTSTANDING MUSIC AND LYRICS FOR "GET'CHA HEAD IN THE GAME"**

**OUTSTANDING DIRECTING FOR A MINISERIES, MOVIE, OR SPECIAL**

Congratulations all around!

# COUNTING HIS BLESSINGS

Corbin's life has been blessed in many ways, and he'd be the first to say so!

## Family

As the saying goes, you can choose your friends, but you can't pick your relatives. If Corbin could, he'd stick with the family that fate gave him. The Reivers clan is tight-knit in the best of all possible ways. They listen to one another, and support one another—through times both tough and terrific. "Each of our accomplishments is a family accomplishment," is the way the patriarch, David, looks at life.

Aside from parents David and Martha, Corbin's immediate family includes three sisters Hunter, who's thirteen years old; Phoenix, who is five; and Jag, who

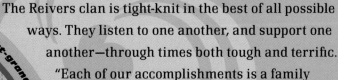

*Baby Corbin with his great-grandparents in Kingston, Jamaica*

"It's about just being grateful for what you have and
not complaining about what you're missing."
—Corbin's mom, Martha

*(Clockwise from left): Hunter, Phoenix, Corbin, and Jag pose for a Christmas photo.*

is three. Each girl has been given the opportunity to try showbiz—commercials, modeling, acting, dancing, singing, whichever might appeal to them. They've also been given just as much opportunity to explore other hobbies and interests.

For a while, Hunter pursued showbiz. When she was very small, she wanted to do whatever Corbin was doing and used to put on little shows with him for the family. She appeared in commercials with her father and brother, but as she grew, Hunter realized that her passions for sports and music overrode her interest in acting. "Hunter is really the jock in the family," says Corbin proudly. "She's played soccer, flag football, softball, and tennis. I love going to her Saturday soccer games and cheering her on. Lately, flag football has become important to her, as well as singing." Hunter is still the Reivers family member who owns bragging rights to having started her career earliest. She had her first print job at the age of three months.

Phoenix is the little sis who Corbin laughingly refers to as Mini-me. "She's just like me," he describes. "She's outgoing, a little ham of

*Corbin with his grandfather Joseph Callari*

an actress and dancer." The youngest of the girls is Jag. She is friendly and gregarious like the rest of the Reivers clan, so she fits right in. As soon as she was born, Martha and David knew that they were blessed with a family full of bright, wonderful children. Just as Phoenix resembles Corbin, he reports, "Jag's like Hunter. So, it's funny. We both have our own little Mini-me's."

An evening out on the town—shades and all!

Corbin is very proud of his kid sisters. He's also very protective of them! According to someone who should know, i.e., *Mom*, Corbin is, "very protective, so much so that at times, he's reminded *me* to watch them or to hold their hands. He's giving me directions for watching them!" Martha laughs. "He'll turn off the TV if he doesn't think Hunter should be watching something." On a more serious note, one day, there was a fire at the school Corbin and Hunter attended. The teachers were trying to get all the children out of harm's way. Martha remembers, "They couldn't control Corbin, because he didn't care about himself, all he wanted to do was get to the kindergarten yard where his sister was—where the fire was—to get her. He just needed to make sure that she was OK."

"He gets a lot of that from us as parents," says David. "We've always been very protective of him, and so, as a family, we are protective of each other." Although Corbin echoes his parents' concern for his sisters and loves to look out for them, it's not all serious older brother stuff between siblings. "Corbin's really wonderful with them," his mom asserts. "He babysits them, plays games with them, reads to them, and does piggyback rides. He's just a wonderful older brother."

*Corbin's family with Tia Kathy and Tia Mercedes*

The girls agree. "He's a great older brother because he's really fun," says Hunter. "We have so much fun when we're together, but at the same time, he can also give great advice. He's always been supportive of the things I've done."

Five-year-old Phoenix pipes up, "He makes me laugh when he pretends to be a monkey sometimes."

Corbin and Hunter dance with their parents at a wedding.

Corbin gives all the props to his parents for the strength of their family unit. "As a family, our thing is communication," Corbin explains. "We've always wanted to be able to be open with each other and to talk about anything. My parents have always allowed me to do whatever I choose when it comes to acting. It was never something that was forced on me. They have always supported me—and reminded me to make sure that whatever I want to do in life is something that I really love and that I am not just doing this for the fame or the money."

His dad has been beside Corbin all his life: coaching, encouraging but not pushing, sharing his triumphs, leading by example, and dealing with whatever disappointments life and showbiz have to offer. After all, David Reivers has lived the ups and downs of the biz (he still does!) so who better than he to be Corbin's life coach? "Dad was able to show me the ropes and at the same time keep me grounded and down-to-earth," Corbin relates. "He's been there to make sure I know that it's not about the Hollywood scene and all that nonsense. It's about doing what you love. We both love acting, and we feel that's what we're here to do." For many young actors, remaining humble and keeping hold of their values can be difficult. But not for Corbin. From the beginning, his father gave him some great advice. Corbin shares that guidance: "People look up to you. They don't bow down to you.

79

Corbin played with sisters Jag and Phoenix when they visited the Utah set of HIGH SCHOOL MUSICAL. "They were out for a visit, and they were really, really excited to see me," laughs Corbin.

*The Reivers family sticks together!*

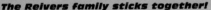

There's a difference." He knows that some celebrities can get caught up on power trips and change how they behave. "They become big, and they feel the need to treat everyone else like dirt because they think that's what they're supposed to do. I see kids treating their parents badly and I think, oh my gosh, if I ever said something like that to Mom…well, it would not be tolerated!" And he would never dream of disrespecting his family that way. Having values and sticking to them, no matter what, comes first and foremost in the Reivers household. "No matter how much money we ever make in life, I don't think we will change our values and how we believe we should raise our kids. It's about respect. You respect people and you'll get the respect back. And that's generally what we teach each other," says David.

"And to be appreciative," adds his mom. "Corbin is very humble. It's not a right, it is not a privilege; what you have is a blessing. You have to appreciate what you have, because that's something very special that not everyone has."

At home, Corbin is not treated like a star. His mom and dad set the standards, and Corbin and the kids are expected to abide by them. His mom explains, "David and I don't necessarily believe in set chores. To say 'You're in charge of garbage' or 'You're in charge of this' is not our way. We've always felt that school was the most important thing, and that's their job above and beyond *all* things. So they are given complete freedom to make sure that all homework is done." Not that Corbin and his sisters never help out at home! "What we say is that if we ask you to do something, then you do it without question. And it's worked for us because I can see with Corbin and Hunter as they're getting older, it's an automatic. If they see a need in the family, they will immediately get up and fill that need."

There are revealing comments about Corbin's true personality from his extended family as well. His aunt Maria Spencer, who acted as Corbin's guardian for a spell while he was in Hawaii filming FLIGHT 29 DOWN, sees her nephew this way: "He's honest and very caring. He has a soul that allows him to feel everything. He's done a lot with his life, but he still has a lot more to go. He's very intelligent, very smart, and very articulate. The main thing is that he's a very passionate person."

Corbin's Tia Mechi says, "Corbin doesn't have any airs about him. He's always done very well in school—I'm very proud that Martha and David have worked to make him so well-rounded. He still had to change his sisters' diapers, bathe them, and babysit. Everything is still the same in that family. Fame hasn't gone to his head."

## Fame and Fans!

Although Corbin has been in the public eye since he was two years old, nothing could have prepared him for overnight stardom!

Since HIGH SCHOOL MUSICAL, his life has changed dramatically. Now, kids all over the world recognize Corbin and company in a flash. "We walk out in the mall, and people know who we are. They start calling our names," he says. "The weirdest thing for me right now is that people know my name. It used to be that if someone on the street stopped me, they would

Signing autographs for fans

81

*Corbin made some lasting friends when he guest starred on HANNAH MONTANA. He got to spend time with Emily Osment, Mitchell Musso, Miley Cyrus, and others.*

ask, 'Are you Chad from HIGH SCHOOL MUSICAL?' But now, people are stopping me and saying, 'It's Corbin Bleu!' I think, oh my gosh, you know my name! And I don't know you."

Corbin's aunt Maria Spencer has also witnessed a change in fans' reaction to her nephew. "When HIGH SCHOOL MUSICAL first came out, that's when he started getting recognized. If we went to the movies or to a store, people might stare, but they weren't sure it was him, yet. But the girls got braver and would come over. Sometimes, he would sit and talk to them. Eventually I had to say, 'Come on, we need to go.' Corbin feels guilty if he can't take a picture with everybody—he wants to, but logistically, he really can't. Not all the time."

He doesn't let it get to him though. He confesses, "I enjoy being recognized because it shows that there is an appreciation for my work. I am a very open, social, and friendly person, and when people approach me to ask for an autograph, I am totally cool with doing that. It is a lot of fun to do."

Corbin acknowledges that there *are* times when being so popular can be difficult. "On the one hand, you feel like you have finally accomplished something, finally gotten to this level where people know you and respect your work. It's just such a great feeling." But, of course, there is a downside to people's interest in him. Sometimes, it can be daunting when he is trying to eat or simply hang out with a friend. For example, "Once, my friend Charlie and I were out to dinner. I had a burger in my mouth, and a group of people came up to me and asked me to take a picture with them. I didn't mind stopping to take the picture, but then more people came up behind them. By the time I finally got back to my burger, it was cold."

*Corbin has remained friends with his FLIGHT 29 DOWN co-stars.*

At the end of the day, Corbin remembers what it was like to be a fan! "If somebody that I looked up to took the time to give me an autograph or take a picture with me, that would make my day. Plus, fans leave feeling really excited and happy. I genuinely enjoy doing it—it makes me feel great that I could do that for someone."

## Friends and Girlfriends

Someone as friendly, handsome, open, and outgoing as Corbin is bound to be popular. He's got tons of friends, both guy friends and girls-who-are-friends, but he doesn't have a serious girlfriend. Nor does he want one—right now. He's got good reasons, the main one being timing. "I'm constantly busy," he says. If he were to start a relationship, he confirms that any potential girlfriend "would deserve my attention and respect—and at this point, those are things that I can't fully give." Corbin adds, "Besides, I'm experiencing life, having fun, and there are so many people out there. Every new experience has something wonderful to offer, and I don't think people my age should close themselves off to that. We are still finding out who we are, what we like in others, and what qualities we don't." Beyond knowing what he is looking for, there is the other challenge of actually finding the person who has all of those qualities—and that can take a long time. "There have been people in my life that I've gotten serious with, in the respect that we really liked each other and dated, but I've never had an exclusive relationship."

What would it be like to be Corbin's girlfriend? Expect respect, that's for sure—and romance! "I'm one of those people who goes all out," he reports. He's a gentleman. He's been raised to hold the door open for a girl, which he finds, "so simple, and yet a lot of people just don't do it. But I've seen,

Corbin and Lauren Storm became good friends while filming in Hawaii.

After HSM wrapped, Corbin and his family visited Circus Circus in Las Vegas and tried a little rock climbing.

with my own parents, it's the little things that count. I'm a romantic. I'm one of those guys who sends roses. I'll sprinkle rose petals on the floor, I'll send chocolates, or take the girl for a romantic walk on the beach. I love dancing and romance." When asked about the romantic moments in his life, Corbin produced a doozy. "Probably one of the most romantic things I've ever done is kiss a girl on the rooftop at midnight under one of the most perfect skies I had ever seen. We were dancing. It was so perfect."

## Qualities He Looks For

The kind of girl that would attract his attention has to have one big thing going for her—honesty. Even when it hurts! "Being open and honest and communicating, being able to talk to each other is the most important thing. In the beginning of any relationship, I want *you* to be able to talk to *me*. I want you to be able to tell me if there's something bothering you, if there's something wrong. If there's anything negative going on, just say it—don't let it swell up inside you and make things worse. It's better to come right out with it in the beginning. That way, we can work on it together and fix it."

Trust and understanding are extremely important, too. "If I'm working from morning 'til night, and there's two days when I can't call you—don't freak out. It's not because I don't have feelings for you anymore, it's really because I just couldn't." Corbin is quick to remind girls that saying you understand while you continue to be angry or pout doesn't count. In order for him to be open with a girl, she would have to genuinely understand and "have faith in the relationship."

He also confides that he would only be able to date someone who has other things going on in her life—things that are important to her

*Checking out DinoLand*

and that she wants to discuss. "I like people who aren't constantly asking questions about my career. I already live that. Besides, it's nice to talk about other things." Plus, if all a girl wants to know about is the celebrity stuff, she may like him *only* because he's famous!

Lucas, Zac, and Corbin in New York City

To find her way to Corbin's heart, a girl must be a friend first. "If you have friendship as a base, you always have that to fall back on if the romantic part ends or just doesn't pan out. I've been very fortunate." When he refers to his past relationships, he is happy to report that he does get along with his exes. "We've still remained friends, and it's been really good."

## Finding the Humor in the Rumors

If everything written online and in the tabloids was real, it would seem like Corbin's dated all of his co-stars. Even though it's not true, Corbin can joke about it. "I've been paired up with everybody: Monique, Vanessa, Ashley, all of them. There was one thing on the Internet saying I was dating Brenda Song. I just think, 'Where do you come up with this stuff? Where do you come up with Miley Cyrus? She's thirteen!' The blogs, chat rooms, tabloids—they come up with the weirdest things."

## The Meaning of Friendship

After family, having good friends is a close second on Corbin's list of blessings. He takes after his mom and dad in this aspect of his life as well; both grew up surrounded and nourished by a circle of trusted friends and confidantes. Corbin feels lucky to have many friends, both in showbiz and out, on the East and West coasts, friends who are guys, and platonic friendships with girls as well. "I'm one of those people who likes to be surrounded by tons of people! Every single day, I can hang out with a different person, or a whole bunch of different people."

The camaraderie he has experienced while filming in both Hawaii and Utah has led to some lasting friendships. "I've gotten very close with all the cast members of FLIGHT 29 DOWN, HIGH SCHOOL MUSICAL, CATCH THAT KID, and HANNAH MONTANA," he says. "I have all their numbers, and we talk constantly. At the same time, I still have friends from high school that I talk to, and two friends from back in elementary school—so I think I have a really good balance between actor friends and those not in the business. I like it that way, because I like to be normal and get away from it every once in a while."

Spending time with friends usually means hanging out at some one's house or going to movies, restaurants, and parties. One of Corbin's best times with his buds was his own fifteenth birthday party. "I had about 70 kids in my house. We had a DJ, a pool table, video games set up on the big screen TV, and it was just insane! There were no drugs or alcohol; it was just kids from high school having fun. The next day at school, everyone was raving about it, saying things like, 'I can't believe nobody drank and everybody had a blast.' That was probably my favorite birthday I've ever had."

Among his showbiz friends, there are lots of kickin' off-screen memories as well. One of the most memorable experiences was when a bunch of kids from HIGH SCHOOL MUSICAL decided to go see Ryne Sanborn—who portrayed the character of Jason—play hockey. "We went to one of his games in Los Angeles," Corbin remembers. "Only in the very beginning of the game, Ryne got hurt, so we all ended up spending the night in the emergency room with him. It was unfortunate, but it shows that we are there to support each other. It was a bonding experience."

More recently, when Corbin was in Toronto, Canada, shooting his new Disney movie, JUMP IN!, Zac Efron also happened to be there, filming his new movie HAIRSPRAY. "We went and we hung out everywhere," Corbin says, "We have a great relationship. It was a lot of fun."

### Who Your Friends Aren't!

Corbin concedes that it's easier to bond with co-stars or keep up with kids from school than to make new friends. Not because he's become less friendly or less

*Farmer Corbin? This city kid tries to be a country boy in South Dakota.*

interested in getting to know other people—it's just that he's learned to be more wary of their motives. "You can't always trust everybody," he says.

"One downside of this business is that it can be hard to tell who your true friends are. People who would never talk to me before suddenly come out of the woodwork and want to be my best friend now." Luckily, Corbin is a solid judge of character. He can tell who is genuine and who only wants to be around him because he is on TV. Whenever he runs into a situation like that, it reminds him how wonderful his real friends are.

Corbin also has to be careful of people who think it's cool to talk about knowing him or any other person on TV. It is not right when people use him to brag to others. Trading on the friendship to make the other person feel important is *not* cool.

*Corbin spends the afternoon fishing in South Dakota. He was there to take his friend Charlie to her prom!*

## What Makes a True Friend

Corbin is totally clear on what a true friend is! Understanding, having his back, keeping confidences, and being loyal are the most important qualities. "No matter what kind of trouble you are having," he asserts, "true friends will always stick by you. They are there to support you, but when you're doing something you shouldn't be, true friends also help lead you in the opposite direction to put you to the right path."

He also knows that insecure, high-maintenance friends just aren't the ones for him. "My real friends are understanding people. They know I'm a busy person and I don't always have time to talk on the phone constantly. We accommodate each other's hectic schedules. Real friends are people you can be yourself around— you don't feel like you have to change yourself for them. They

*Signing autographs at a Make-A-Wish Foundation event*

know who you are and love you for it." Keeping confidences is a biggie for the Bleuman. Especially because, for some reason, Corbin tends to be the guy that others pour their hearts out to. He finds himself frequently giving relationship advice to worried friends. While he likes being helpful, he acknowledges that he wouldn't seek outside advice for a relationship of his own. "If I'm in a relationship and I tell you something, it doesn't need to be everybody else's business. It's between the two people, and that's it. It's about trustworthiness."

## The Gift of Faith

Strong family values, true friendships, and all the other amazing gifts that have been given to Corbin wouldn't be possible without a deep spiritual life as well. Corbin's very passionate about his faith. "I pray. I think that's what has kept me going all these years when it comes to overcoming obstacles. When I get very nervous or self-conscious or stressed, or I'm feeling burned out, what keeps me going is feeling that God has His plan for everybody. I can't control it, or fight it. Once you learn to accept that He has His plan, it helps you, because even if you're going through problems, you just know that everything happens for a reason. Kids go through a lot of rough periods, and I wouldn't think of trying to force my own personal beliefs on others, but if I can lead by example, by being respectful to everybody no matter what...that feels good."

Corbin recognizes that people may look up to him, so it is important for him to be a solid role model. He is happy to show others what an incredible life he has led and wants to let people know that his many blessings come not only from his own hard work and perseverance, but from what God has given him. "We're Christians. We respect everyone; whether we agree with certain lifestyles or not, it's never something we shut down. Even the Bible says you're not a judge of others. God's the judge. Your job is to show people the power of Christ through love and show them what an incredible life you can lead and the happiness you can have when you have that comfort of knowing that there's somebody there. Anytime you feel alone, God's always there. He will *never* abandon you—ever."

## The Gift of Giving Back

If it's true that it's better to give than to receive, Corbin has reason to feel especially good! He's blessed to be in a position where he can help others. It's probably the best "use" of his celebrity. Whether he's helping family, friends, or fans, or pitching in to raise awareness and funds for those less fortunate, Corbin tries to bring a smile to the lips of everyone he meets. Corbin's agent Bonnie Liedtke says "what impresses me most about Corbin is that even with his amount of fame, he is the same boy he was years ago. Dependable and honest, he's always the first to help out with charities." He offers his name and fame to several charities, but the one he campaigns for most is called The Starlight Foundation.

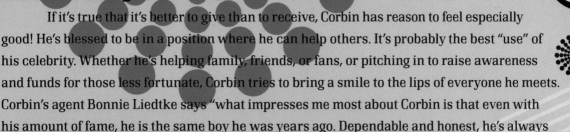

*Thanksgiving at the L.A. Mission*

The Starlight Foundation was created to give kids with chronic or terminal illnesses a day where they're having so much fun, meeting stars, going to amusement parks, having parties, or participating in activities that they actually forget that they're sick. As an ambassador of the organization, Corbin explains, "We set up events that we bring the kids to, and it's great. There are games and tons of kid celebrities to meet. At other times, we go to see them at the hospitals and, it's really incredible …and heartbreaking." It can be especially hard to see kids that are so similar in age to himself or his beloved sisters facing devastating conditions. "When I meet these brave kids, sometimes I think, 'That could be me. That could be my sister. That could be anybody.' It tears you apart to see and hear about the things they go through. Sometimes you see them sitting there, and you know they're going through something awful, but when you walk in the room and just talk to them, you can see them get happier. You know you're doing a good deed, and man, it makes you feel so good."

Even if he had never been on screen, Corbin would find a way to give back. He encourages all of his fans to find a way to make a positive impact on the world around them. Not only does helping others benefit a cause, it feels great inside. "That's why all of us volunteer. We go and do whatever we can. Because we see the huge smiles on their faces, and when you walk away, you just know you've just made their day."

**With Steven Anthony Lawrence (left) at a Make-A-Wish Foundation event**

# WHAT'S COMING UP

On the set of JUMP IN!

JUMP
jump roping productions ltd.
Corbin Bleu

**"HIGH SCHOOL MUSICAL has opened a lot of doors for me."**

HIGH SCHOOL MUSICAL 2 and the Disney movie JUMP IN! are just two of the doors he's decided to walk through. And they aren't the only things he's got going on!

## HIGH SCHOOL MUSICAL 2!

First, of course, is the highly-anticipated sequel to the hottest movie in Disney Channel history, HIGH SCHOOL MUSICAL 2. As of this writing, the entire cast will be back, and the story will unfold over the summer—meaning the HSM kids won't exactly be in high school. Instead, most of them will be spending the summer at a country club, which Sharpay and Ryan's grandfather happens to run! You can rest assured there will be fun in the sun, even more chart-topping tunes, and maybe a couple of surprise romantic moments, too. The cast gets back to work on HIGH SCHOOL MUSICAL 2 in January 2007, and the sought-after sequel should be hitting TV screens (and iPods) near you in spring 2007.

### JUMP IN!

Another hugely exciting piece of news on the Corbin front is the brand-new Disney Channel TV movie, JUMP IN! In this touching tale, he plays a young boxer-in-training named Izzy

*Corbin and his father on the set of JUMP IN!*

Daniels, and his co-star happens to be the very best actor Corbin knows: his dad. David plays Izzy's father, a retired famous boxer who once won the Golden Gloves championship.

During a break from work, Corbin gets to catch up with friends.

"Izzy comes from a long line of boxers," Corbin explains. "His dad and his granddad were both champions of the Golden Gloves, which is an annual tournament for amateur boxers. Izzy's been training his entire life for a shot at it and makes it through his final exhibition match to qualify." Izzy will need to train intensely to win in the ring, and he means to, only he gets sidetracked when a cute girl asks a favor. A group of girls on Izzy's street are known as "Double Dutchers"—that is, they compete in double Dutch jump rope competitions. When one of their members drops out just before the championship, leaving them without enough jumpers to qualify for the competition, one of the girls is desperate enough to beg Izzy to fill in. He decides to accept the offer but of course doesn't tell his father or his fellow boxers, who'd be horrified. Once he becomes a "Double Dutcher," the real drama begins.

While working on the film, Corbin attended a competition and was awestruck. Corbin marvels, "I went thinking it was just little girls jumping rope and singing, but it's a real sport. You see people flipping and jumping over other jumpers— just doing these incredible gymnastic moves that are hard! They do these tricks in the air that'd be hard enough to do outside the ropes—never mind actually performing these stunts while jumping, not missing a step within the ropes or tripping over them!"

After HIGH SCHOOL MUSICAL, Corbin landed some guest-starring roles in TV shows, and there will certainly be many more. In this pic, he's all decked out for an appearance on NED'S DECLASSIFIED. "I got to play a 'thespian' and it was really funny. I played Ned's nemesis. My character was a bad guy, but he was a pathetic bad guy. He wasn't even scary evil—just kind of stupid evil. He thought he was suave and was always trying to steal Ned's girl. The role was a lot of fun!"

David Reivers says, "Working on JUMP IN! with Corbin has probably been the high point of my career. I've never had anything better, not only because I'm getting to work with Corbin, but we have great material. It was rewarding to get a good role, playing his dad, and besides, we had a wonderful crew up in Toronto, where we filmed the movie. Everyone was so friendly and professional that it made the experience that much better."

Corbin echoes his dad's sentiment. "It was incredible having my dad there. After every scene, I'd look to him for the thumbs up, wait for his approval because I respect him so much as an actor. Usually he'd say I did fine, or great even—but every once in a while he'd say that I needed to do something differently or change something in my delivery." Corbin says that the natural chemistry he has with his father made a lot of the scenes flow easily, and it will make the film that much more real for the audience.

For JUMP IN!, Corbin had to learn a bit of boxing—and a lot of double Dutch! Both were beyond strenuous to learn! Being a dancer who loves a challenge, Corbin went at it full-force. "It was intense training—but really great," he says enthusiastically. "I actually want to continue boxing, because it's just the best workout I've ever had in my entire life. You do weight training, push-ups, sit-ups, and circuits. Then, like in MILLION DOLLAR BABY, you learn to punch the speed bag and the heavy bag, work inside the ropes and out of the ring—even skipping rope, which helped for the double Dutch training! You come out of there dripping, like you jumped in a pool. You're tired, since you've worked every muscle, but you feel so great afterwards!"

The love interest for Corbin's character is played by Keke Palmer from the movie AKEELAH AND THE BEE. The pair got on well as friends off-screen, and it's a good thing they did,

*Like father, like son: Two talented actors take on boxing in JUMP IN!*

92

*Corbin in the ring*

because they had to do a kissing scene. "She actually has to kiss me in the movie and it was her first kiss *ever*—on- *or* off-screen," Corbin relates. "So she was freaking out a little."

For Corbin it wasn't a big deal, it was just another scene—he talked to Keke as a big brother. "I kept telling her not to freak, it's really nothing—it's just your job, it doesn't mean anything. And when you have your first real kiss in real life, you're going to have butterflies in your stomach and you're going to be extremely excited. This won't be like that! This will be just like another day at work." Keke appreciated the advice, but she still refused to rehearse the kiss with him! Corbin tried to tell her it'd be better to try it first without the crew, cameras, the director looking on—that it'd be less nerve-racking, but she didn't want to. "It was really funny. But we had a great time."

Beyond HIGH SCHOOL MUSICAL 2 and JUMP IN!, Corbin is looking ahead to acting in more movies. "Eventually, I'd like to do a horror movie, an action flick, a drama, a comedy. I want to be well rounded and do all types of movies," he admits. If there's a dream film Corbin has, it might be an up-to-date movie version of his favorite book, THE GREAT GATSBY by F. Scott Fitzgerald. "I just love the story," he says. "It is a love story, but not too sappy. It's got a lot of symbolism, too."

Corbin's proud agent Bonnie Liedtke forecasts a very bright future for him. "Watching Corbin grow up on- and off-screen has been a joy. I believe in my heart that Corbin will go very far in his music and acting career. I look forward to seeing him as a leading man and stealing the show!"

*Corbin in the studio working on his first album*

## An Album!

Trouble with singing? For Corbin, that's a thing of the past! Corbin conquered his fears by dialing up the right mental attitude *and* putting in the time with vocal coaches. Pushing himself to do the best he possibly could has paid off in at least one big way: He's signed with Hollywood Records to make his own solo album.

When recording executives from several companies heard "Circles," the song that Corbin recorded for FLIGHT 29 DOWN, they were immediately interested in signing him. It all happened so fast that Corbin began to wonder if he could put together an entire CD with songs as good as "Circles." Corbin confesses, "Everybody loved this one song, but I'm nervous about everything else. And I know that there's no reason to be, but it's still there. There's a lot of expectation, which is stressful." Or was. "Then I suddenly had this epiphany," Corbin divulges. "I was just like, all right, I just need to just dive in and have fun making the album. If I'm so obsessed with making it perfect—because I am a perfectionist—it's not going to work for me. I need to not worry about that and just have fun."

Corbin describes his music as a mix of R&B and pop, "like Usher, Justin Timberlake, John Legend, or even the male Alicia Keys, because I will be playing piano on it." The CD is another reason for Corbin to look forward to 2007—movies and music will be his New Year's one-two punch!

## Corbin Bleu, M.D.?

Aside from showbiz, Corbin has a few other ideas about his future. For a straight-A student who excelled in math and science, it's not so surprising that he used to think seriously about becoming a doctor.

*"In more than ten years of being his agent, I have never seen Corbin without a smile on his face," says Bonnie Liedtke.*